Autumnia

Three Novellas

Autumnia

Three Novellas

KEITH DEWHURST

GREENHEART PRESS

First published in Great Britain 2023
by Greenheart Press

A CIP catalogue record for this book is available from the British
Library

ISBN 978-0-9571829-6-7

Produced by The Choir Press

Cover Design by Paul Baker of A Stones Throw

KEITH DEWHURST was born in 1931 and worked in a cotton mill and as a travelling reporter with Manchester United before becoming a playwright. Three of his seventeen stage plays were premiered at the Royal Court Theatre and six, including his adaptation of Flora Thompson's 'Lark Rise', at the National Theatre. He wrote two movies, eighteen TV plays, of which 'Last Bus' won the Japan Prize, and episodes for many series, including the original 'Z-Cars'. He was a Guardian columnist, a member of the Production Board of the British Film Institute, Writer in Residence at the Western Australian Academy of Performing Arts and a presenter of TV arts programmes and a Granada comedy show. He has written two football books and co-wrote (with Jack Shepherd) a theatrical memoir.

Contents

Autumnia

PROLOGUE

Malcolm had been on the razzle for thirty-six hours when in a pub near Earl's Court he met a girl who said that she could get him some more Benzedrine. But she disappeared, and he had to drive back to the Squadron. The wrong M.O. was on duty, the older one who disapproved of stimulants. Old Horseface was the next best bet, but he had been shot down the night before, and nobody knew where his stash was. He took it with him, said popular opinion. Or maybe the batman stole it, said Vesey, as the crew wagon jolted them out to the Dispersal Point. Whichever it was, Malcolm had sat through the Briefing with pricking eyes, a fixed stare, and the feeling that his head might roll off. He had a quarter of whisky shoved down his boot, but could not risk a swig until he was inside the aircraft. It gave him the energy to go through his checks and to take off, and after a few more gulps they were over the sea and Vesey said "How are you?" on the intercom and Malcolm said "Right as rain, dearie," and felt it. He noticed everything in a magnified way: smells of glue and leather, the luminescence of his dials, hums and rattles of metal, the whisper of his silk undergarments, the thickness of each of his three pairs of gloves, the stink that came up the piss-tube attached to the control column. The time and the stages of the journey passed quicker than he ever remembered. He heard his crew over the intercom but their voices seemed far away and nothing to worry about. Indeed, there was nothing of any sort to worry about. He was in command of his aircraft, his mind, and every inch of the surface of his body. He floated, in the perfect world of the sky. Then ahead of him flares exploded. They were red and yellow, with cascades of secondary bursts. Malcolm knew what he had to do. He turned the aircraft to fly along the alley of lights. The crew shouted that the flares were scarecrows and not the real pathfinders. It did occur to Malcolm that, at the end of the display, beyond the yellows, there should be a succession of green markers, but with the clarity that had been his all night he knew the explanation. "Master Bomber's been shot down, dearie!" he yelled. Vesey argued. Malcolm ordered him off the intercom. Vesey struggled out of his Engineer's seat and ducked into the cockpit with a map-frame in his hand. Malcolm pushed him away. They both shouted but neither pressed his intercom button. A sudden hard brightness dazzled them and Malcolm did hear Vesey and someone else cry "Bandit! Bandit! Bandit!". They were caught in the fighter's landing lights and Malcolm began a climbing turn. There was a sound like thrown gravel. Bullets going through the aircraft, Malcolm knew. That proved it. Scarecrows be damned. "We're over the Big City!" he screamed, hitting out at Vesey. Then an orange flash blinded him and smoke stank. The windows splintered and freezing air sucked at him, as cannon shells blew the front turret and two men to pieces. It was a familiar tactic, Malcolm had time to remember: one night-fighter scared you with his lights, and his partner sneaked in to shoot you up.

ONE

Mercy Runacre sat up in her four-poster reading *War and Peace*, which she was sure she would never have attempted but for the fact that Russia had been brought into the War on our side. She wore bedsocks, a pair of her husband Hector's pyjamas, a lacy bedjacket bought in Paris in what seemed a different lifetime, and a khaki scarf. This had been knitted in the Village Hall by Lizzy Tuffrey's half-wit daughter Lupin, and it was so loose and skew-whiff that Mercy had decided not to pack it up with the rest, even if they were only for Barrage Balloon Crews.

"It's the wrong colour for the Air Force boys," Mercy told sallow Mrs Tuffrey. "I'll keep it on one side until we send our box of goodies to the Commandos."

Such habits of command were in her blood. Runacres had owned the village since 1649, when they bought it in the sale of Cavalier lands that financed Oliver Cromwell's invasion of Ireland; and because Mercy had been the heiress Hector changed his name to hers when they married. Before that he had been Hector Sugden, Q.C., a surname that Mercy perpetuated by giving it to her house spaniels. The Sugden of the moment was banned from the bedroom, but lay nevertheless at her feet: better, she opined, than a bottle, because he did not lose warmth in the night.

This mattered because the room itself was unheated. Old Tilly came in every day, and Mr Witford worked outside, but the village girls had gone, to the Forces or factories or the Land Army, and Mercy herself had too many responsibilities to have time to hump firewood upstairs every day.

She had to keep up morale in the village and write letters to the two local men captured at Dunkirk. She was on the County's Ambulance, Civil Defence and Land Army Committees. She dashed to London whenever she could, to attend higher Committees, and keep some sort of check on the house in Uppingham Gate and Hector's laundry there, and on what remained of their social life.

She corresponded with people it was impossible to meet, although so much of their news was bad, and above all she had the children; and all of this to be done in a war, to rhythms and feelings that nobody controlled and nobody could stop.

She read now of Napoleon at the gates of Moscow, and the Rostov family's evacuation of their home, and she knew how well the story was written because she had experienced something of the sort herself. The military had commandeered the Hall, and every day Mercy saw how they damaged it. She lived in the Dower House, which had stood empty for years because her mother was in a private mental hospital: mind disease ran in her family: was it a failure to be interested in life?

In her haughty good looks and lean body Mercy resembled her father, but feared that her emotions were those of her mother. Would her own mind, she wondered, be similarly obscured? Would she recognise its weakness? Her mother's self-control had become suppression, Mercy thought, so that whatever was undesirable ceased to exist. Yet control was still better than chaos. Look at these evacuee children who had screamed and run riot, and then most of them gone home when the London bombing stopped. How Mercy had loathed them, and at the same time wished them well.

With a start she looked up. Hector had appeared from his own room. He was in his shirt-tails, which showed his long legs to advantage. You don't look like a Sugden, she thought: but then, neither does the dog, and I know how your dick springs up like a subaltern's sabre. Hector had good cheekbones and mouth that a woman arching back could imagine to be cruel, and there was always a stillness about him.

"I say, Mercy," he said, "you wouldn't mind joining me for a spell, would you?"

"You can't want me naked, Hector. Not in this weather."

His arrival from London had been without warning, when she was already in bed with the Rostovs. There had been a flask and a sandwich in the car, and his driver was on a camp-bed in the dining-room.

"I thought that it would wait till morning but there won't be time. I must have your opinion about something."

He sat on the edge of her bed.

"The fact is," he said, "I've been asked to stand for Parliament."

"Parliament?"

He shrugged.

"But it's wartime."

"Poor old Harry Mulville," he said.

"Oh," she said. "Aren't you cold?"

She pushed her dressing-gown at him, like a rug.

"I won't get elected. Harry's majority was too big."

There was no need to elaborate. They both knew the constituency, and what was hoped for it, and why Hector had been asked to take time off from his job in Civil Defence Control and campaign.

"Who tipped you the wink?" asked Mercy.

"Attlee," said Hector. "He chaired a meeting I was at this afternoon."

Golly, thought Mercy. Attlee himself, using coalition government time to promote a little party deal. Gosh and golly.

"There'd be a selection process," conceded Hector. "But I'd hope to come through that and reach the actual hustings; although with eggs being rationed I wouldn't expect too many to be thrown."

The cruel mouth withdrew into its shy smile.

"If I said yes how far would you feel able to help?"

An immediate response died in her mouth. Thoughts raced and her stomach stirred. There were many things that each of them could have said, but it was wartime, and the new Britain that would be built thereafter. They had their duty, and so many people would always have more to complain about.

"Of course," said Mercy. "Of course, darling. I'll do whatever I can."

In London the next evening, Hector returned to the house in Uppingham Gate to find among the post a letter in an Air Ministry envelope. It regretted to have to inform him that his son Pilot Officer Malcolm Runacre was missing in action, presumed killed, his aircraft not having returned from an operation over Berlin.

TWO

Call it a sixth sense if you will, but Mercy had always been right about her children. A fear of bad news may have dulled her for more than a year, but when Hector telephoned at midnight the effect of his news was the opposite to that she had expected. Instead of a blow whose ache would last forever she felt joy and liberation. At last the War had released her. She was free of it; which was consistent, she realised.

Had she not known the sex of all four of her children when they were in her belly? From the way each kicked and wriggled she had known that Malcolm would be perfect, and Rufus sickly, Magnus a more impetuous and sillier version of his father, and Henrietta a perverse and dreamy little girl. And she had always known when they were in danger.

She had insisted, during the infamous holiday at Walberswick, that Rufus's flushed lassitude was a sign of something serious, and she had been right, and thereby saved his life.

Then again, a mere week ago, she had seen one of her better omens: ducks on the lake, noticed anew as joyous smudges of colour against the mist and ice. Something good would happen, she had been sure, and so it did.

Magnus telephoned that very evening, to say that he had wangled the posting he wanted, a Staff job in what he called a pretty hush-hush corridor of the War Office. He was safe for the duration, thought Mercy, and, knowing him, she was sure that he would amuse people and blunder into more good luck.

So it was with absolute certainty that she reassured Hector on the telephone.

"Don't worry, darling. Our Malcolm's alive. I'm sure of it. I've never been more certain in my life."

Next morning she told Henrietta, who was three years old and did not react. She fiddled with her porridge spoon, and her questions about Malcolm came at intervals over the next twelve months. As for Rufus, he was sixteen and his public school was evacuated to the country. Mercy left a message with his housemaster, and Rufus called back later.

"Are you lonely?" he said. "Do you want me to come home?"

He would always think of her first, Mercy realised, and even though she had saved him his love and his polio limp made her feel guilty, somehow, and she felt easier with Magnus, and his ridiculous absorption in his own affairs.

"Let me see what I can discover about chaps who come down in the sea," had been his response to the news, as though a subaltern yet to turn nineteen could command what information he chose, and Mercy laughed inside herself, at the notion of having produced such a creature.

Phyllida Mace was her next obligation, and she approached it by telephoning the mother Lady Mace.

"Oh my dear. Oh how awful. Oh poor, poor all of us."

"I'm certain he's safe," said Mercy.

"Is there anything at all I can do?"

"I'm not sure how to find Phyllida. She was bombed out, wasn't she? I think I'd better come to see her next week."

*

9

They met for tea at the Dorchester, which Mercy's mother had adored from the day it was built, and her father thought vulgar. The lounge was shabby and cigarette-smoky, and there were American officers with smart prostitutes.

"I'd have asked you home," said Phyllida," but it's tiny. Malcolm only just fitted in."

She smiled at her brave little joke. She was an energetic, fairish girl with a square face and a deep laugh, but today she seemed lethargic.

"I don't suppose there's any better news?"

Of course there was, said Mercy, and showed the letter from Malcolm's Commanding Officer. Phyllida read that Prisoner of War Cards could take months to arrive, and Red Cross confirmation of casualties even longer, and that as far as could be gleaned from the briefing of the returning crews, Malcolm's aircraft had dipped out of the formation at some distance from the target. It might even have gone down over Occupied Territory, in which case anyone who parachuted could have fallen among friends. There was it is true little real hope, but it would be wrong to deny any at all, especially in the case of so resourceful an officer.

"As you see," said Mercy, "it reinforces my feelings absolutely. And we'll visit the airfield."

"Can you do that?"

"Hector can arrange it."

"What about the rest of the crew?"

"What about them?"

"Well: what's the news?"

"There isn't any. When there is we'll be in touch with their families."

They stared at their tea. There was toast, and paste sandwiches, but no elaborate cakes.

"You knew all those crew boys, I suppose," said Mercy.

"Yes."

Phyllida seemed about to say more but did not. She was in naval blue, and a translator at the Admiralty.

Mercy waited. Bomber crews had leave every six weeks, and Malcolm had spent his last one with Phyllida, driving from London to his final mission. Mercy had hoped to be told about him, but the girl seemed wooden and evasive, so in the end Mercy asked.

"He was marvellous," said Phyllida, "Absolutely marvellous. Look, I'm sorry, but I really do have to go."

Malcolm had ducked away from the girls his mother had hoped he might like, and fallen in with this one during the single year he had spent at Oxford. She was brainier than Mercy would have wished, and poorer, the daughter of a man who had been knighted for services to medicine. Now Mercy wondered what she was hiding: another boyfriend no doubt. Why not, she surprised herself by thinking. It was difficult to choose at the best of times, and this was a War, so that the future seemed blank.

Phyllida smiled, and showed her better side.

"I've got some of his things," she said. "But I'll keep them, if that's okay. Give them back when I see him."

Brave girl, smiled Mercy. Very correct. Very urbane. They understood one another she thought, and paid the bill.

In Uppingham Gate the tall houses looked weary. The railings had gone and there were Fire Brigade tanks in the gardens, and rubble where two houses had been bombed. There was a smell of drains and burning and old mortar, and there was dust everywhere, no matter how much clearance or rain: dust on the vestibule floor, dust on the letters that lay there, dust on surfaces and objects: the dust to which bombs had reduced many buildings, or shocked and loosened from ones that seemed undamaged: and there will be dust under my naked bum, thought Mercy, when Hector comes home and I have him make love to me on the half-landing.

THREE

It had been Hector's innermost fear, when he read the letter from the Air Ministry, that he and his wife would lose as well as a son their sexual spontaneity, and he had felt that sense of nothingness in the penis that is the opposite of an erection's demanding swell. Had they not lost the knack before, when Rufus was ill with polio?

Lust is primeval, but so are grief and guilt, and woman's instinct that men are savages and should be kept away; and a man who is happy to be kept away cannot be the embodiment of the mystery; he cannot possess the phallus and the seed to which submission must be made, and after their Rufus shock it had taken them two years to recover their selfish excitement.

Hetty was the careless product, conceived in Paris and born when her mother was forty. Then in the War Mercy and Hector saw less of each other, but despite their tiredness protected their lust. "Stay in London," she would say when she felt weary. Now the letter had come, worse than the blow of illness, and Hector's fear was the reason he had waited for hours to telephone her.

But to his surprise she glowed when she saw him, and was demanding, and for as long as that continued, for as long as they had a happiness despite it all, he allowed her to believe what she wanted.

He challenged nothing. He seconded her hope, and after a month or two their families, and friends who had been concerned, behaved as though the matter was resolved. Malcolm was alive. Word would come. He had parachuted to safety and was a Prisoner of War.

Nothing shook Mercy, or the atmosphere around her, not even when they went to the Bomber Station to collect Malcolm's belongings, and to talk to his friends. They did not need to do it and in fact it was forbidden. Belongings were packed and sent on. New people moved into dead men's huts.

But Hector had both status and a history: in 1915 he had enlisted in the Royal Flying Corps, and been an observer and artillery spotter over enemy lines. He was shot up, crash landed, and after hospitalisation given a desk job. The Station Commander was sure that Mercy's self-control would be equally officer-like, and offered lunch in the Mess, where Hector's Western Front anecdotes were much appreciated.

Afterwards the Station Commander drove his guests to look at the quarters, and introduced them to Jenkins, who had been Malcolm's servant. He was a Welshman, an ex-miner, small and knobbly and shy.

"We liked Mr Runacre," he said. "No side to him. He'd have a game of darts with me and Charlie."

"Who's Charlie?" said Mercy.

"Oh, sorry, mum. My oppo, mum. He does the next hut, like."

As the Station Commander led them away Mercy turned back to give Jenkins ten shillings, and Hector, waiting, had a feeling that they were being watched. He turned in time to see an airman duck into a hut and gasped, because it was Malcolm. Then he realised that it could not be.

Their poise held through the winter and into 1944, when in March Hector fought the by-election and was defeated; but he knew that he would stand again in a General Election at the end of the War. The constituency was a railway town in the Thames Valley, part rural, part dormitory and part engineering, and Mercy was a triumphant canvasser. She took Hetty with her and the local paper wrote about her hero son who was in a German prison camp.

Then the spring in which white-starred vehicles lined every road became the summer of the invasion of Europe, and of the German flying-bombs and rockets, which made Hector's Civil Defence duties arduous again, and brought the village a confusion of voluntary evacuees.

Later, when schoolboy Rufus was a man and looked back, that summer and autumn seemed a curious time, apart from the before and after. Newsreels showed the liberation of Europe. Tanks edged through ecstatic crowds, girls clambered on to the turrets to be kissed and groped, flowers were waved and thrown; and still the Germans fought their nihilistic rearguard, and rockets fell faster than sound upon London, the explosions first and then the screech of the descent.

Life's pattern was exultant but crazy. It had to alter, and it did, when Hector learned through channels that a member of Malcolm's aircrew had been located in a Prisoner of War camp.

His name was Vesey, but no family or friends had met him, not even Phyllida, because he was a replacement for the familiar Flight Engineer who had been wounded by flak fragments on the night that Malcolm's flying-suit was torn to shreds and he landed the aircraft on two engines, to be cited for his medal.

The Station Commander had moved on by now, but Mercy was on a Red Cross committee and used her contacts to trace Vesey's widowed mother. She lived in Fulham and Mercy visited her. There was no-one to look after Hetty and so she went, too, the first time she had ever visited London.

Its vast dinginess on that day would loom always in her memory, as would the unused smell of Mrs Vesey's front room, the chill and slipperiness of the linoleum, and the fact that Hetty herself was tiny and had bent down to look under chairs and along skirting boards, and realised that the cat had excreted behind the horsehair sofa; but Hetty was too unsure to mention it.

When she did tell her mother afterwards she was commended for her tact, which made her sure that secrets were a good thing, so that she kept to herself the fact that the lacy cover on Mrs Vesey's milk-jug had a bead-bobble missing.

Mrs Vesey herself worked in the box office of the Walham Green Empire, and was neat with a take it or leave it sort of manner. She had received a pro forma Prisoner of War card which was definitely from her Fred because she recognised the writing.

Mercy revealed that she had taken the liberty of writing to Fred herself, to which Mrs Vesey gave a brisk little nod. She added that Fred's last letter before he went missing had said that he was very happy with his new crew and that the Skipper was a regular daredevil. But she did not show the letter, Hetty realised when she thought about it later, and her mother had not asked.

They went home on a Number 14 bus, along the Fulham Road to Knightsbridge, which was a wonderment to Hetty, who never in her later life thought that the route was as interesting as it had been when buildings were smashed and there were balloon-crews in the parks and uniforms everywhere.

"Did you like Mrs Vesey?" asked Mercy.

"I don't know."

"People like that have had to struggle. We must always respect their pride in themselves."

Some weeks later Mercy received a reply from Vesey, but it was also a Prisoner of War card, and said nothing.

FOUR

Religion had been a formality for the Runacres, the confirmation, as it were, of the eternal order in which their place was an important one. At the same time they had a very clear idea of what was meant by the words Decent Behaviour, and Mercy herself had strong moral impulses which if asked, and it was poor form not to do so, she would have called honest-to-goodness Christianity: for example, she did send to the Commandos the misshapen scarf knitted by Lizzie Tuffrey's daughter, because why was an idiot's offering of less value than that of the Lady of the Manor?

For Hector the spiritual was another matter. His father had owned a chemist's shop in Stockport, and his grandfather had been a mill overlooker and a chapel sidesman. Hector was a self-created lawyer but something of the evangelical, of the millenarian, of the Lord's breath blown into muck to create soldier saints, still rumbled in his vitals. Why else did he wear the Labour Party's colours?

Well, there were personal prejudices, of course: against some of Mercy's friends who treated him with amused smiles, and against grandees of the law and civil service who did the same, when he remembered better men in the provinces who had nothing. He was unaware that to most people he seemed to have more icy grandeur than the grandees, just as they were unaware that behind his manner he was a habitual emotional questioner. Would people hear the vowels that betrayed his Northern origins? Would his sex life fail or not – because it was sex between he and Mercy, and not social climbing as everyone thought? And now, he wondered, would Mercy herself turn to religion over this mystery of Malcolm? One colleague's wife, on the death of her son at Anzio, had spent thousands on spiritualists. What would Mercy do, in what way would her composure crack, when the fact that Malcolm was dead could no longer be avoided?

Yet was he dead? Why was there no report on the finding of his body or, so far as Hector knew, of any other member of the crew apart from Vesey? There was not even an accurate notion of how and when the Lancaster had gone down.

To know more Mercy, seeming to be deep in village life, would wade in and ask her contacts all kinds of favours. So would Magnus, as far as he was able. But Hector had more reticence, not least because his situation, as he nursed his prospective constituency, was more delicate.

Already, he realised, people around him were beginning to

think about what would happen after the War, and so was he. And it was not just what would have to happen to create in England the New Jerusalem. It was one's own career and possibilities. Civil servants treated him with more caution, and he was more selective himself, and went out of his way to freshen old legal contacts.

There were men he could have pressed for information about aircrews and prison camps but he did not. Better now to avoid moral debts, and besides, what difference would it make to the eventual facts? None. Although it might well agitate Mercy. He persuaded himself that this was why he tried not to broach much with her. But he knew that Magnus telephoned her every week, so he bought him lunch at the club, to glean what he could.

It was a chance to pontificate, and Magnus seized it. Prudence. Await events. No news is good news after all. Time is a great healer. Who knows what might happen? I don't say this openly to Mummy but I'm sure that I allow it to occur.

He's a youth, thought Hector. Why does he sound middle-aged?

Magnus went on to discuss himself. He wanted to go to the Inns of Court. Follow in your footsteps, old pater. I've inherited your forensic cast of mind.

Hector foresaw at once that Magnus would have early success and then stick in his groove and become a bore. There were eccentrics of that sort in most chambers and if they had a bit of money, as Magnus would, they more or less blundered along.

Because Magnus was his son Hector voiced none of this; but he did make appreciative grunts, catch the eye of a club servant, and order two more glasses of the Dow. It hadn't run dry, thank God, even though where they sat in the Morning Room the windows were boarded up and the curtains wrecked, having been blown out twice in the last ten days.

*

Then it was another Christmas, which they spent at the Dower House, and drank a toast to Malcolm, wherever he was, and attended the midnight carol service, to which Mercy took Sugden because the farmers were allowed to bring their sheepdogs. Malcolm's name had been on almost every Christmas card they received. In the spring Hetty joined the infant's class at the village school, and soon after the War in Europe ended. Within days the Air Force sent Missing Personnel Research Teams into Germany.

News came sooner than they hoped. Two members of Malcolm's crew were buried in a village cemetery in sandy, wooded country a hundred miles west of Berlin, as they had been warned might be the case.

Where had the aircraft come down, asked the investigators. Had anyone seen it? Was it on fire? Did it make some sort of a pancake landing? Where had Vesey been taken prisoner?

There were no easy answers. Vesey had landed in the village. The two dead men had been found by a roadside, their parachutes half-open. The plane itself had not come to light, although some people claimed to have heard an impact. Like many an aircraft in those situations, it might have fallen into woodland or a small lake: a place where no-one looked, or where it was hidden, half-buried, submerged who the hell knew where, or cared in these crazy times?

What had been found, on a heath amid burned-out flare-cases and strips of anti-radar foil, was an open parachute with no man in the harness.

When she heard this Mercy was excited. Her speech became more rapid. She asked again and again whether they should tell people about the mystery parachute, or keep it to themselves until there was more news. Hector advised caution: in his heart he feared that there might never be more news: the investigation would move on to other villages and crash sites, and after a few months its teams would be disbanded. The tide of Mercy's emotions worried him. It was sweeping them apart, he realised.

If Malcolm was alive he would appear. If he did not they must mourn him, but Hector was not sure how they would do that, after years of insistent optimism.

Then one day a lawyer friend who was in the Allied Control Commission told him how German war criminals had disappeared, or become other people, or if they were useful to Military Intelligence had new lives invented for them. Might there not, Hector mused, be many others among the displaced millions who craved reincarnation? What if Malcolm was one of them?

He racked his conscience for reasons why Malcolm might despise the life that he had led. How well had they known each other? How well had Hector been known to his own father? Not at all after the Western Front, he thought.

Shell shock. Loss of memory. Suffering so unbearable that it obliterated everything. Suppose this had happened to Malcolm. Or a blow to the head, an injury that made him forget who he was.

Why have these thoughts come to me now, worried Hector. Had they ever occurred to Mercy? Why was she so ecstatic about what she believes? Has she never reckoned the actual likelihood?

He did not ask. Her trance enveloped him. They were strangers who lusted for each other. In armchairs, in the back of the car, in copses of the exhausted-seeming spring her orgasms said everything.

Then a letter came from Phyllida. It said that she was sorry and prayed that they would understand, but in the natural course of things she had met someone else and was engaged to be married.

"Phyllida's interesting," opined Hector, "but I never did see it as a long-term recipe."

Mercy disagreed. What Phyllida had done was a betrayal. It changed everything, and meant that Malcolm needed a mother's love all the more. They must go to Germany themselves and find the aircraft.

"My darling, have you any idea what it's like over there?"

"You can get us the permissions."

"I'm not sure that I can."

"In a couple of weeks you'll be a Member of Parliament."

"Mercy, I may not get in."

"Of course you'll get in."

"Our canvassers say it's touch and go."

"Nonsense."

That night Hector went to Mercy's room and began to pull off her nightdress. Her nipples were hard but she resisted. Hector was rough. She twisted and struck him. Hector hit back but the spaniel Sugden snapped at him. Hector pulled back. Mercy was wrapped in the eiderdown. Hector touched her hair with the back of his hand, like a stupid blessing, and went away.

Two days later, Vesey's letter arrived at Uppingham Gate. Hector knew that he should read it to Mercy over the phone but instead he invited Vesey to lunch at the club, where plaster-work was still down but the windows had been refitted. Vesey was dark and neat and had oiled-down hair and a moustache, and Hector was surprised to see that he was an officer, not a Flight Sergeant.

Vesey read it, and with a flick of the eyes said "They made me up, sir. I'm a Regular, see?" He grinned at his own other ranks' tone. "Went in as a Boy Apprentice. Like a lot of Flight Engineers."

"What'll you have?"

"Same as you," said Vesey, playing safe.

"Are you with the old squadron?"

"For a kiss and a wink," said Vesey. "Then I take up this new posting."

"So you've caught up with an old face or two?"

"They told me you'd been down there," said Vesey, and came to the point. "Is there any news?"

"I was hoping you might tell me."

"Malcolm talked about his mother," said Vesey. "I suppose she's not allowed in here?"

"She's in the country."

Hector watched Vesey's interest in him fade. The man had come not to help, he realised, but because he was curious. Then their drinks arrived and they said "Cheers," and were silent until Hector persisted.

"You think he's dead, don't you?"

Vesey did not look him in the eye.

"Do you know that he is?"

Vesey struggled with himself. Then he took a breath, and described how they had been lured by scarecrow flares into a nightfighter trap, and how the front of the aircraft was shot off and he and Malcolm had sort of fallen out. How else could he describe it? That's what they'd done. They'd fallen out. And, unlike the target where it could be as bright as day and there were fires and explosives and flares everywhere, this had been countryside and dark. Vesey's chute had drifted him into a farm pond, actually, not as luck would have it a very deep one.

"So, really, you've no idea what happened to Malcolm?"

Vesey's gesture meant that other chutes could have blown anywhere.

"But he was alive when you fell out of the plane."

"Yes."

"So if he did land it couldn't have been all that far away from you, could it?"

"Not in theory. No."

They had gulped their drinks but Hector did not want to break the mood by ordering new ones.

"What's your guess? That his parachute never opened?"

21

Vesey began to speak but stopped himself. Then he surprised Hector by looking at him with wide open eyes: an appeal for help, and an admission that the man was out of his depth.

"Malcolm didn't *send* you to meet me, did he?"

It was one of those questions that came of their own volition, and had made Hector such an unnerving cross-examiner.

"No," said Vesey, and seemed about to panic. "Bloody Christ no!"

"He's disfigured. Is that it?"

"No. I mean – No. How would I know?"

Vesey had begun to sweat. The questions had confused him, Hector realised. They had told him something that he would think about later, but which at the moment neither he nor Hector could disentangle. In a courtroom Hector would have probed. But he was in the club, amid cigarette smoke and confident voices and the glances of men who thought "Poor Runacre! That business of his son, I imagine!" He was with a man who might well have hoped to tell him in the gentlest sort of way that Malcolm could not be alive and that his body, like thousands of others, might never be found.

"Actually," said Vesey, "I could do with a Jimmy Riddle."

The next time Hector went to the club it was as a Labour Member of Parliament in a landslide victory that had surprised him, although he could not imagine why, and for every man who shook his hand there was another who avoided him; and sitting in a cubicle of the lavatory he overheard a conversation at the urinals in which he was described as a traitor to his class. Whatever that is, he replied to himself.

When they lived above the chemist's shop in Stockport there had been jerries in the bedrooms and a privy in the yard. Later they made the great move, to a row of chunky Edwardian villas that faced an unmade road and open fields. There was a walk along hedgerows to where the tram drivers changed ends at the terminus. It was his younger sister, sent away to school, who had brought Mercy into the provincial equation. Hector wiped

22

himself, stood and shrugged into his braces, so that they raised his bespoke trousers again.

Two weeks later, Malcolm came home to Uppingham Gate.

There had been a phone call, and then breathless messages from Mercy to the House of Commons, and attempts to get everyone together. But in the event Magnus was sent to Berlin by the War Office and Rufus was on a long-arranged visit to a friend in Scotland, so that it was Hector, Mercy and Hetty who waited in the house that smelled of bomb-dislodged mortar.

At the sound of the bell they ran to the hallway. They heard his feet grate and saw his shadow cast by lamp-light onto the frosted glass that had somehow survived on one side of the door. Then Hector opened the door wide, and there was the familiar big hunched shoulders and a grin. His hair was different and he had a scar, and wore a demob suit with a flamboyant red silk scarf instead of a tie.

He smiled at Hector, whose shoulder he gripped with his left-hand, in a gesture of taking charge, and even in these moments and at her age, Hetty saw her father depleted. Then Malcolm went to Mercy. She held him off for an instant, to search his eyes and face, and then they were together in one mass, she was crying out as in sex and he incoherent and snuffling.

Hector and Hetty watched. The door was still open and they were not sure what to do. Then Malcolm more or less disengaged himself and said "Hetty? Little Hetters? Gosh and golly! How are you?"

"Hail Prince Leafmould of Autumnia!" cried Hetty.

"What's Autumnia?" said Malcolm, sweeping her up with one hand, kissing her, and putting her down again. "One of your storybooks?"

Mercy's laughter was hysterical, and she bounced up and down in front of him, like a girl, and Hector closed the door and they went upstairs to the drawing-room, except that Hetty stood for a moment in the hallway, immobilised by the weight of her new secret.

FIVE

"Your scar," Mercy could not help saying, "the scar on your face," and she touched the shiny vellum burn marks on his hands. He held back, as though remembering that he had once been in agony and afraid to move. They asked him questions at the same time and Malcolm blushed and ducked his head. He did not want to re-live things, although he knew he must.

It was the falling from the plane, he began, the pure perfect freedom and the bliss of seeming to float, whilst at the same time chilling air rushed past. It was the supreme experience of his life. He did not want it to stop but knew that it must, and pulled the ripcord long after he had been trained to do. The others had already opened their chutes, he supposed, and been blown miles away.

He's found himself, thought Mercy. When he went away his sensitivity was hidden but now he can show it. They would share it, she knew, share it most gloriously, when before that had been difficult.

"But where did you land?" said his father, ever practical. "Where were you held prisoner?"

Some things, Malcolm had to confess, he did not remember. His chute had landed him on heathland, and for the rest of the night he had walked westwards, so far as he could judge from the stars. When daylight came he'd hid under a hedge and slept. No-one found him. At nightfall he walked again but by this time he had eaten his chocolate bars and ditchwater made him feel queasy. He could not keep going and wandered into a village, where the postmaster arrested him.

Policemen were sent for, and he was put on a train, to be taken to the nearest Offlag. The train had to wait in marshalling yards, where it was bombed and set on fire. Malcolm's memory of the next months was patchy.

He remembered a civilian hospital but that, too, was bombed, and he found himself in a camp of Russian civilian captives who worked on a construction site. Conditions were bad and people died. When the Germans realised that Malcolm was English they pulled him out; but because his papers and clothing had been destroyed he could not prove his identity as an officer, and they sent him to an ordinary Stalag. It was in Bavaria, and he worked on a farm.

By this time Germany was falling apart, and there had been no letters or parcels or contact with the Red Cross for months. Eventually their guards ran away. The prisoners stayed where they were until the Americans arrived.

"That was months ago. You could have told us. Not that we didn't know that you were safe."

"That's it, you see," said Malcolm. "That's it. All I wanted to do was to stay hidden."

"Hidden?" said Hector.

"It's safe."

Mercy could not stop herself.

"But darling, you aren't in danger anymore."

They watched him. There were tears in his eyes. Henrietta's mouth was wide open. Malcolm tried to speak. How harsh these electric lights are, thought Mercy. How stale this furniture seems, how distant and meaningless its associations.

"I've no ambition," said Malcolm. "There isn't one thing in the world I want to do. I just need someone to look after me."

Hector knew that he should take charge but could not.

Mercy cried "Come along! Come along! What are we all doing? It's bed for Henrietta-boots and then grown-ups supper!"

She told Malcolm every scrap of news about family and friends and people in the village.

"What about old Brookie?" he said, meaning the London housemaid.

"Gone, darling. I think that servants are gone forever. Don't you, Mr Labour M.P.?"

"I suppose so," said Hector, and had a mental glimpse of the Dower House washerwoman Lizzie Tuffrey, not so much deferential now as uncertain how to behave in a new world.

Mercy rattled on about War Work and how it had been exhilarating, in a way that she would be glad to forget, and Malcolm said, "Sorry. But I'm drained. Can I go to bed?"

Sorry, they said. Sorry, darling. Thinking of ourselves. But it's all laid out for you. You know where.

He went and they were silent. Hector waited. Because she was vindicated there was a change in her. Then as they washed up like robots she exclaimed, "My God! I forgot to tell him about Phyllida!"

"Won't it keep?"

"No, Hector. It won't."

She ran up two flights of stairs shouting Malcolm's name and when he appeared in an old dressing-gown that looked stupid and boyish she said "I'm awfully sorry, darling, but Phyllida went and got herself engaged."

"Phyllida?"

"Phyllida, darling. Didn't you spend your last leave with her?"

"Of course," said Malcolm. "Of course. Phyllida. Yes. Well. She was just a chum, really. Not much more."

He gave a hurt little smile and shrugged. He reads me, she thought. He has a radar like whatever it is that stops bats from flying into trees.

"You're safe now," she said. "I'll take care of you. But you always knew I would, didn't you?"

Hector was still in the basement kitchen. He bent over the table in his shirtsleeves, like a manservant, and read the evening paper. She sat opposite him. Neither spoke. Then Hector got up and poured two cooking brandies. He chinked his glass against hers and drank.

"The fact is, Hector," she said, "that if there's no sex in it I can't bear to be near you."

She was wearing flat heels, a tweed skirt that emphasised her stomach and hips, and a square-shouldered shirt-blouse whose formality made Hector want to rip it off and expose the remembered body beneath: the sharp brown nipples, the little puckers of her belly that showed not so much her age as the experiences of a woman who has lived. But his desire censored itself and he said "Same here. I can't stand it, either."

Her smile was wry. "Sorry about that."

"So am I," he said, thinking: it's what I learned from you: brisk honesty: except that it's not, really, is it? He began to shuffle plans in his head but she forestalled him.

"I'll go to Estoril," she said. "Would you mind?"

"With Malcolm?"

She gulped her brandy.

"Why," he said, "are we so clipped and civilised?"

"What else is there?"

She tossed her head. The habit of command, he thought. He sighed and undid more waistcoat buttons.

"What about money?" he worried. "Exchange Controls. All those stupidities."

"I've got all I need over there, haven't I?"

It was true: the villa built in halcyon days by her maternal grandfather, the investments he made, the other properties. Then Hector said: "What about Hetty?"

"I'll take her with me."

"She's at kindergarten."

"There's a convent school down the road. Then she can come back and board."

He was non-plussed.

"Oh come on, darling. You know what it's going to be like

in this parliament. You're already knee-deep in all-night sittings."

It was true: and since to his astonishment he had been made a junior minister, and thrust into the very thick of the government's battles, Hector was busier than at any other time in his life. To be free of a small child would be a boon, at least until they had broken the back of their civil servants' resistance to the legislation. All the same, he thought. All the same.

"But you will hope to come back?" he probed.

"High days and holidays, darling," she said. "Speech days and State Openings."

She twinkled at her own deftness and held out her glass: "Any more?"

Hector poured.

"What shall we tell people?" he said.

For a half-breath she was caught out. Then she shrugged.

"We'll tell them the truth," she said. "Malcolm's nerves have been shattered by the war. He needs to rest in a beautiful place."

SIX

Belle Epoque and square, with icing-sugar stucco, palm trees, gravel, steps to the portico, shutters for the winter and in summer canvas awnings, the villa in Estoril had been willed to Mercy when she was a child by her maternal grandfather Frank Hindle, whom she never met.

Hindle was the son of a Pennine handloom weaver, and when he was a boy saw soldiers chase men who tried to destroy mill machinery. He could write and do arithmetic and tramped to Manchester, where he became a carrier's clerk. Then he worked in the railway goods office and scrimped and saved to start his own cotton waste business, but lost it when trade fell off. But

Hindle always believed in himself, and in his late twenties his luck came in.

He had an older friend who worked in a bank and the pair of them saw what would happen at the end of the American Civil War Cotton Famine. The friend contrived to syphon money from dormant accounts and they bought a bankrupt factory.

By the time the fraud was discovered they had made a small fortune, and the bank accepted the resignation of its clerk, its money back at interest, and the maintenance of its reputation. Then the erstwhile clerk died and Hindle bought out the widow.

His own wife was plain, watchful, competent and had a sharp tongue when she used it. Her first married home was a Manchester cellar, the last, where she died early of a breast tumour, a dark stone Lake District mansion that looked through wet rhododendrons at occasional bright water. Hindle did not remarry.

He brought his widowed but childless cousin Alice to keep house. The boys were at boarding schools and he sent his daughter to an expensive place in Eastbourne. They made friends with privileged young people, had the cash to keep up with them, and lost their Northern vowels.

When his daughter married into the squirearchical Runacres, and saved them with her money, it seemed to Hindle a job well done and he retired. One son wandered around Italy on an annuity, the other was happy to assume the business. Hindle himself bought the villa in Estoril and never saw England again.

"He was always a rum bugger!" said know-alls on the Manchester Cotton Exchange, and suspected deeper motives.

They were not wrong. Hindle had met in London a Portuguese woman, the wife of a diplomat with whom her sexual life had ended. But they were sound friends, and the diplomat was delighted that his wife had found a person who, however uncultured, was forever curious and of a worldly-wise humour. Hindle moved to Portugal, and took Alice with him to keep house.

She wore black, and panted in the heat, and made cakes for

the garden fetes at the English Church. But she would not attend the Services because she was an old Methody, and when she was a girl had seen moorland women whistle and stamp themselves into trances.

"Santa Maria!" said the Portuguese lady, when Hindle told her this.

She had questions but Hindle affected not to know the answers. He preferred to be tacit.

But winters were kind, English money went far and Lisbon was at hand, where the lady introduced him to the opera and the scandals and politicking of the backward but once imperial little nation; and once a month he would meet the diplomat in a café, to discuss property and investments.

Then one year he knew that he was ill. He went to Madeira for a couple of winters but it made no difference, and he died in the presence of Alice and the diplomat, who were his Executors, and was buried in the English cemetery.

His family were not informed until it was done, and were surprised that his Portuguese estate had gone to his grand-daughter Mercy, with the proviso that Alice had an annuity, and might occupy the villa until her death. Not that they cared much. They had inherited plenty, and were on the crest of the great 1908 cotton boom. They built another vast mill, its water tower decorated with a dome like an Indian palace, and re-doubled their share values.

Mercy herself was a child in Belgravia, unaware of her investments, and Portugal was not mentioned because Colonel Runacre hated dagoes. So Alice was unmolested, through the Great War and into the Twenties, when Estoril enjoyed its moment of deco chic, and, because it was cheap, accommodated exiled royalty.

So, too, Mercy's first adventure as an independent woman was her visit to Alice. Her impressions were strong and she confused them with later occasions. The light on the ocean when she woke up, horse-drawn carriages, the Romanian who had a heart attack in his deckchair, the day the cat killed baby finches, the visit from the retired opera singer who had known Verdi, her own realisation that the decay and overgrownness of the villa conveyed a sort of wisdom about the passage of time – were these memories of that first visit, of her second when she went with her brother to bury Alice, or of her honeymoon with Hector?

Certainly the night club, the casino and the shimmering backless dresses were with Hector, who refused to go there again because the regime was a dictatorship. Even so, she knew, he had liked the slowness of life and the deference, the sense of living in an earlier Europe.

Hector had asked her about Alice, of course, but she said little. It was all so different, she said. Alice had been fat and sweaty and closed the shutters as well as rolled down the awnings, and her accent mixed thick Lancashire with hectic Portuguese, so that she said 'losh' instead of 'loss' and 'Weshton-Shuper-Mare', and 'Conishton', where she had first kept house for Hindle.

"But she surely went to bed with him?"

All Mercy knew, she replied, was that Alice went to bed early with her cat and a bottle of white port, and that she was suspicious.

"Shushpishioush?" grinned Hector, who had a friskier mind when he was young than he did as he grew older.

"Suspicious," repeated Mercy. "So she never told me any secrets."

This was the first lie she had ever told Hector and at the time it was an instinct, and she did not know why. All she knew was that getting away with it thrilled her.

As time passed she withheld more and it seemed to her that Hector realised and was glad for her secrets, the outward form of which he sought in her moans and shudders and ready vaginal wetness. So his desire was continuous, and his refusal to engage with Portugal kept his left-wing credentials spotless. Yet at the time of Munich he did look up from the paper one breakfast time.

"If war does break out," he said, "it could be difficult for people with property and so on overseas."

He smiled, shook the paper open again and said "My God!" at the announcement of some legal appointment.

"My God indeed," thought Mercy, and wrote to her lawyers in Lisbon.

Hector's advice, which he never again mentioned, proved timely. Britain took many assets held abroad, to pay for the war, but the Estoril villa was saved, enmeshed in Portuguese holding companies, and if Mercy felt any guilt she assuaged it by sharing what other luxuries she commanded.

Her many hens laid eggs, when other people had to scramble that ghastly powder, and whenever Hector returned to London he took country things as gifts: herbs, fruit, vegetables, cheese, illicit meats, paper bags of cut lavender, honey from the Vicar's hives.

Once he was taking a rabbit he had shot to a friend in Regent's Park and in the West End, minutes after the bomb fell, saw many precious stones winking in the rubble of a jewellers.

"Don't go for them!" people shouted. "Don't risk it!"

But one man did and the rubble collapsed around him, and Hector saw his brains bashed out. He told Mercy and it was on her mind for months.

At the end of the war in Europe there arrived a fat letter from Lisbon, and when Malcolm came home, and Mercy and Hector sat in their London kitchen, Estoril rose up in her heart as a solution.

SEVEN

Because Magnus was serving in Occupied Berlin, Mercy announced her departure with a cheery letter. "Fly South when you can, darling!" said the P.S., knowing that he would not be able to. Rufus was at Harrow, so she went up and had tea in his study, and traded without remorse on the fact that he loved her above everything.

"I simply have to do it, darling. I know you'll let me, because you're the one person in the family who *understands* about emotions."

Crippled Rufus blushed. He had never thought to hear her say it.

"How bad *is* Malcolm?" he said.

"In pieces," she confided.

"Can I come down to see him?"

She hesitated.

"We were never tremendously close. Did you realise?"

"If I did I couldn't say anything, could I?"

"I mean, he's not boring like poor old Magnus or anything but—"

Rufus stopped. She looked older, he realised. Faded, like so much after the War. Yet her cheekbones were still marvellous and her blue eyes like Heaven, and her confidence thrilled him.

"It's just that with everything that's happened Malcolm and I might find more in common now," he said. "We might even help each other."

Mercy studied him. Behind his pain he's a stubborn little sod, she realised.

"The trouble is, darling, we'll be off before your term ends. I simply must move swiftly."

There was hurt in his smile but he gestured it away. What he cared about most was her love.

"Of course you must," he said. "Follow your feelings. Of course you must. For all of us."

*

Rufus had grown into his own person, Mercy thought on the way home. Because he was crippled and could not exercise he was already overweight. He was soft and unaggressive and comfortable, as though despite the fact that he was barely eighteen everything was decided. Look at how well his trousers were pressed, not at all like a schoolboy's flannels. And his study could have been a room a hundred years ago, with its cut flowers and souvenirs and walking sticks. His was the life she had saved, after all, and it had a familiar sentimental surface. But she was no longer sure of what lay beneath. Rufus might hurt her, she thought, and neither would see the danger until too late.

Mercy's other visit of the week was to her mother, who sat in the nursing home's conservatory with her hat and glasses on, and a rug over her knees. She recognised Malcolm at once.

"Hello, Malcolm, dear. How's your mother?"

In vain Malcolm indicated Mercy.

"No, no dear. That's not your mother. That's the almoner."

Mercy described this visit to Hector and he said "Power of Attorney. You must speak to the others."

"I don't have time."

"Telephone."

"I'm needed elsewhere."

"It is most vital," he said, "that someone holds her Power of Attorney."

Silence.

He shrugged. He was making notes on government papers: the re-drafting of a Nationalisation Bill.

"You think I'm bolting, don't you?" said Mercy.

"Other people will. I know that you can't help yourself. It's something that can't be denied."

On the train to Portugal, in the sleeper between Paris and Irun, Mercy felt intense excitement, an almost breathless sense of joy and freedom. Then Hetty was sick, and the attendant had to be called to change the bedding.

EIGHT

Malcolm's knees were bent by the down-crushing force of the youth's embrace, and from his mouth that was plundered by the other mouth came choked whimpers. Then he did sink to the ground, and tear at the buttons of the boy's cheap trousers, and take out the dark thick stick of a penis and fold his lips around it.

Mercy watched from the top of the villa's marble stairs. At her side Hetty stared for another moment, scrutinised her mother, and then went on bare feet to her bedroom.

The youth must have heard the faint slap-slap because he turned in a lazy way and Mercy saw that although he had the coarseness of a waiter or someone of that sort he was not unhandsome. Saliva and, she thought, a dribble of blood ran from his lips and his big white teeth. He smiled. His eyes flickered, slow and shadowy. He was unabashed. His movement made Malcolm look up, see Mercy, and grin. I should turn my head, she thought, but I can't.

"Sorry, darling," said Malcolm, "It seems we couldn't wait."

She trembled and at the same time wanted to laugh.

"Shouldn't you introduce us?" she managed.

"Federico. My mother. Mercy."

"Don't tell me. He's a barman."

"Shrewd," conceded Malcolm. "Almost there. I said you would be. Actually he's a washer-up at the Palace Hotel."

"That's not where you met him, surely?"

"On the beach, darling. After dark."

Federico re-arranged his clothes, wiped his mouth, and made a little upright shrug.

35

"Of course," said Mercy. "Of course. Do come up and have a drink."

It was the evening hour, when the water was steely, the sunset glorious and the breeze brought a refreshing chill. Thin sweater time, she always called it. Hetty came from her room in a dressing gown and shook hands with Federico as though nothing had happened. She sat and watched and was given a cocktail olive. Malcolm made drinks. Compared to Federico he seemed to lumber, Mercy thought, but she was serene because of what had fallen into place.

A hundred incidents in Malcolm's youth and friendships were explained, a hundred suspicions justified, a hundred questions raised that might never be answered, and aches and irritabilities and flushes of guilt that would never be assuaged.

What had a woman done, to create a man who was not a man at all, she wondered. It unnerved her that he was as bold and able as another female, but she basked in the fact that he loved her, and was a soothing or a gossipy companion. As for Federico, she knew already that here was turmoil, and that for as long as possible the three of them would have to avoid a return to England.

NINE

As a child Jack Marland had rickets and now he looked older than his thirty years. He stooped, his joints stuck out, his mouth was thin and his cheeks were grey and hollow. Many pushier people dismissed him because he was so unashamed a provincial, and ascribed the fact that he did not say much to a lack of confidence. His shrewdness and his gleam of humour they missed, all too often because it was at their expense. Hector had met him in the Tea Room, liked him, and taken him as his

Parliamentary Private Secretary. Now, because their driver like half of those in the pool was off with flu, they trudged from the Commons to the Ministry.

"Bloody silly to drive short distances anyway," said Jack, "even if the work is killing us."

Everything was grey and dirty: slush, patches of ice, unpainted buildings, war damage, fog that hung around the street lamps, half of which were turned off anyway because of the fuel shortage. Hector's feet were cold and he had a cough. No coal had arrived at Uppingham Gate for two weeks, and he slept with an eiderdown rolled around him, and two pairs of bedsocks.

Jack stopped. "Well," he said. "I'll get off at Edgehill!"

A dead sparrow lay on the pavement, its feathers filthy, its legs stuck up and spiky.

They halted. Hector shrouded the little corpse in his breast-pocket handkerchief and placed it in a rubbish bin.

"Edgehill!" he echoed, their useful shorthand for what could not be altered, and out of respect they paused.

Then they smiled at themselves and trudged on.

Roddy Wigham, the Permanent Under-Secretary, was portly, with a red face, metal spectacles and a grin. He came in on the train from Haslemere and was a fellow member of Hector's club, where he specialised in mock indiscretions about the proceedings of the Bridge Committee.

"I apologise for the wattage," he said, indicating the bulb whose light was as tired as the afternoon gloom, "but it's the Minister's latest insistence."

"We know," said Hector. "It was that or the corridor radiators. Jack persuaded him to get off at Edgehill."

"You keep saying this," said Wigham. "Would it help if I knew what it meant?"

Jack explained. Wigham's clerk sniggered. Wigham himself protested that they last time they used the phrase –

"Clause Thirty Seven B," interrupted Hector. "Did your wizards come up with the cost deferentials?"

Wigham motioned the clerk to hand out copies. Hector hated figures. He sighed and tried to look firm.

"As you see, Under Secretary, and as we did warn the Minister, the sums involved in compensation are substantial. But a political necessity, one presumes."

Necessity, thought Jack. Having walked across the Pyrenees to join the International Brigades he had seen political necessity: factory owners driven out and shot: nuns beaten up: later, having taken a bullet through the lung in the Battle of the Ebro, he was declared unfit for British military service and spent the war as an Air Raid Warden and Billeting Officer: work at the grassroots that helped him into Parliament.

He realised that his mouth was open, and that Hector was staring.

"Comments, Jack? Footnotes? Words of warning?"

"None."

He remembered blood from the mouth of a Moorish prisoner someone had kicked. And here he was, in the place of power and compromises. His wife was dead and his daughter with his sister in Oldham.

Later they were telephoned by the Whip's Office. The debate had taken a turn for the worse. Procedural votes had been forced. They must return to the House. Hector sent a doorman for a taxi, and in the back of it said "Once upon a time, in the exultation of victory, I sat on the bog at my club and overheard Roddy Wigham at the urinals. He called me a traitor to my class."

"Class?" said Jack. "Class? You don't have a class. You're a lawyer."

"No class?" grinned Hector. "Aren't you supposed to be a Marxist?"

"It's seeing more of life," said Jack. "It confuses me."

TEN

The debate went hammer and tongs until midnight, for the most part blowy rhetoric about what people were or were not entitled to expect. Afterwards Hector sat in the bar with a whisky. In the War he had found energy, but in government exhaustion; and unlike when he was in court, he did not feel that he was being himself.

But who was he now, he wondered as he sat there, his thoughts so intense that no-one approached him. He had let Mercy go because he loved her. He lived alone. Who was he? Then a Messenger muttered in his ear that he could have the Minister's car if he wanted it.

"Many thanks," said Hector, knowing that the Minister must have walked into Pimlico, and the basement flat of the woman he believed to be his total secret.

At Uppingham Gate the lights were on and his son Rufus, still in his duffle-coat and college scarf, fuzzily asleep on the drawing-room sofa.

"Rufus? What's happening? Aren't you supposed to be in Oxford?"

"Golly," said Rufus. "Oh, Christ. What time is it?"

His eyes were puffy, as though he had been crying.

"Rufus what are you doing here? What's the matter?"

"You know what I'm doing here."

"I don't."

"You bloody will know what—"

"Rufus, please—"

"Oh for Christ's sake!"

Have I deserved this, thought Hector. Have I deserved a youth in this state?

"Pull yourself together," he said, and at once regretted it.

Now Rufus did blink tears, his cripple's pudgy face soft and soggy.

"Dad, why are you doing this? What's happening to us? Why are you like this?"

"Like what?"

Rufus threw a cushion. He looked weak.

"Sorry," he said. "I'm sorry. It's because I love you."

Hector sighed. He hated this. On the other hand, he knew what was happening.

"What's this about?" he said. "Has Magnus been after you? Is that it?"

Rufus nodded. That was it. Magnus.

"You know what he says, don't you?"

Hector knew.

"He's telling everybody. Everybody we know."

"He's hurt," said Hector. "He's jealous of your mother's attentions."

"But if he loves her like me he should—," Rufus began, and then blurted, "He said the most awful things about her. He thinks she's gone mad."

"Do you?"

Rufus hesitated.

Then he said that what had been amazing was his trip to Estoril in last year's Long Vacation. He had never seen Mercy so happy or so handsome.

"Of course, I realise why they can't come back," he said, "and of course I understand about them, and about you and mother. Of course I do."

In fact he did not, absolutely, but hoped that if he said that he did Hector would treat him as an equal and spill some information.

But all Hector said was "What about Malcolm?"

"What about him?"

"How close do you feel?"

"Well, I never really knew him before, did I? I was ill for years and then he went to the War."

Hector calculated the evasion in this reply and said, "Nevertheless – you did rebuff poor old Magnus?"

ELEVEN

After his unpleasant little reunion with Malcolm, Magnus had gone first to see the wartime flame Phyllida. She was affronted by the way in which he tried to shove past her into her little mews house, and banged and bolted the door against him.

Magnus continued to shout, at which Phyllida's husband, who knew the story and thought that her evasions on Malcolm's behalf had been foolish but honourable, went out in his ex-navy white rollneck sweater and said, "Look here, Runacre, I won't have my wife called those names!"

Magnus repeated them. Phyllida's husband feinted with his fists and kicked Magnus hard on the shin.

A passing delivery boy twanged his bell and shouted, "Fair's fair, guv! Marquess of Queensberry!"

Magnus limped away. He knew that he was obsessed but did not care. It was because he saw through people's self-deception and knew better than they did themselves what they should do. Someone once said to his face, "Your charm's won this!" but it wasn't charm: it was common sense and directness, which he had put to good use when he traced Malcolm's squadron servant Jenkins.

Magnus went to the Rhondda, where Jenkins was a colliery clerk, knocked on the door of his terraced house and explained himself in a penetrating voice.

Jenkins was flustered, and a woman inside shouted "What is it?". Jenkins closed the door on her and walked Magnus up the street. The woman looked out, still questioning, and from the lamplight Jenkins made her a gesture of reassurance.

"I was never a part of it," he insisted. "Never a part. It was Mr Runacre and Charlie. But I respected them, see? Grand chaps in their own way, they were. Both of them."

Magnus produced money. Jenkins said he didn't need it, and even if he had he wouldn't take it.

"All I needed," said Magnus, "was your confirmation."

"Well, you've got it," said Jenkins, "and I hope you feel as bad as I do."

Vesey, posted overseas, did not answer his letters, but after the Rhondda Magnus knew that he could no longer evade the nub of the thing, and went to the Fens to hunt down Charlie Slater's past. It was a cold and dispiriting journey, trains late and connections missed, and when the taxi from Ely Station reached the tied cottage in the middle of a flat and colourless nothing, the earth frozen, the cart track treacherous, the leaden light becoming night, the driver did not want to wait and made Magnus haggle.

Then after half an hour a hunched figure came up the track, a lump of dark out of the darkness, sacks tied round his overcoat, and in mittens, a balaclava and gumboots.

"Mr Slater?" said Magnus, and began to explain himself.

Slater was suspicious but lit oil lamps and opened the flues of the range that had been banked up all day, so that the cottage was at the same time damp and overheated, and uncleaned and untidy but easy. The curtains had been hand-made with love, and the rugs on the flagged floor chosen with care.

"Can I see Charlie's room?" said Magnus.

"Threw it all out when his mother died," said Slater. "Damned stupid it was. Purple bed cover. Silver paper round his what-nots."

"What-nots?"

"Picture frames. Threw it all out."

He was down to his braces and flannelled shirt and had eased his boots off. He held out his cup for another swig from Magnus's flask.

"Might I use your lavatory?" said Magnus.

"Outside privy. No light. I'd piss on the ground."

Magnus did. His urine drummed on frozen mud. There was steam.

He let the driver drink from the flask and went back inside.

Not that there was anything he could say. Charlie had gone on a twenty four hour pass to London and been killed by a flying bomb. His mother died of cancer two years later.

Magnus had lied, of course, when he said that his brother was still unaccounted for. "I seek out his friends and people who knew him," he said. "I suppose that it's laying him to rest."

Slater guessed that he was lying, and thought he knew why. He grunted. He wanted to be left alone.

There was a photo of Charlie and his mother on the dresser, and Magnus knew that he should take it at all costs, but could not. He scrutinised it and said nothing. He poured more whisky into Slater's cup. Slater nodded. He had rough but dulled good looks. Charlie's were the real thing, Magnus knew.

When he took his discoveries to his father and brother their refusal to listen maddened him. Be civilised, they said. Accept it. Do nothing. But he was dizzy with it. He wanted to shout it in his mother's face. He thought that he would explode. He drank in the daytime and neglected his studies.

The result was that he failed his Bar exams, and his situation became one that he could not endure. He needed to know who he was and be respected, and he was neither. He went back into the Army, on a seven year commission, and was posted almost at once to Malaya.

TWELVE

At Oxford Rufus was a boy among men who had returned from the wars. Winters were cold and his disability earned him rooms in College, a ground floor set which he shared with a thirty year-old named Evans, a clerk turned wartime officer who wanted to become a teacher, and had earned a place through a demob grants scheme. A tutor hoped that the two might help each other, but they did not blend.

Both socialised little and worked hard, Rufus because he was steady but slow, Evans because he knew it was his chance. Each, when in a fury of concentration, resented the presence of the other.

Rufus was considerate and would often limp upstairs to a library. People he had known at school tried to boss him and told him to assert himself against a prole like Evans, even if he was older. But disablement made Rufus different from men of his own age, and his youth could not share what an Evans, in the Pay Corps, had experienced in war.

Rufus respected such experience and did not push. He had a huge capacity for intimate association but could not bring it to bear. He had learned patience in physical things and had a vivid sexual imagination. Later in his life women of all sorts would trust him as a confidant, but this had not happened yet, because he did not believe that anyone would want to engage with a cripple.

He had no intense friends, then, but acquaintances to whom he joked that he would be fine when he grew up. He liked places where he could stare at girls but did not have to talk to them.

The prettiest were in amateur dramatics, but most of these people seemed show-offs. He went to the Labour Club – indeed, his father came up to speak – but the fact was that most of the girls of his own background were with the Conservatives, an organisation both social and political.

One evening at the start of his third year he went to a talk given by a Tory shadow minister whom he knew as one of his father's legal cronies. Rufus knew that early and disastrous attempts to grope girls in the library had given him a mixed reputation and was not surprised when he was snubbed by two, greeted warmly by one he did not know, and found himself unable to hold the gaze of Rosemary Richards, whom he had stared at for two terms but been afraid to approach.

She had a taut figure like his mother and a confidence in her Midlands accent and provincialism that he wanted to see crumpled and made sweaty by his caresses. Her bones were strong, her hair scraped back, her mouth curled and her eyes a brave blue. Her clothes were plain and her shoes clumpy. She talked over people and had no particular graces.

She was pushy, said the snobs, but they were daunted by her even as they smirked. She described her father's small-town plumbing business, and how workmen were lazy and customers did not pay on time; these stories became examples when she questioned a guest speaker about exchange rates, or taxation as a disincentive.

Rufus could not get his mind off her. He knew that he could influence her, and make her smoother and more formidable. But all he read in the way she dealt with him was disdain. She observed his confusion. She saw that there was more to him, but all she said was why was a man like his father in a Labour government? Oh, and that smart clothes were a waste of time. She'd sooner spend the money on a European cycling holiday.

So it was a surprise when at the buffet after the talk, and he had swapped some chaffing remarks with the speaker, he found himself unable to move away because of the angle of Rosemary's stance.

She wore a fluffy jumper and a heavy scent. Rufus inched sideways but the table-edge pressed into his thigh. Rosemary held a plate of Russian salad in one hand and hooked the other into Rufus's fly buttons.

He blushed and said "Ah!" The speed of his erection was as great as its discomfort.

He tried to grin.

"Invite me to tea," said Rosemary.

"Yes," he managed.

She stepped back with a dreamy smile. He contorted himself to get his penis into a more sensible position.

Everyone noticed, he thought. But they had not. They laughed and brayed about their own concerns.

"Don't buy jam," said Rosemary. "I'll bring some of my mother's. It's superior to all this shop rubbish."

On the afternoon appointed for tea Rufus asked Evans to work in the library, but out of curiosity Evans hung around, until Rosemary said "Excuse me, but do you always pick your nose?"

Evans wanted to hit her but skulked out. Rosemary ignored the incident and said that she knew about Rufus's family connections, and was it true that he had been promised a job in the cotton business if his tripos results were good?

"Head office," he affirmed. "Manchester. Research."

"But even if you fail," she said, "what are they going to do? Chuck you out into the street?"

Scales fell from his eyes. She has the courage to face facts, he thought. I've always dressed it up in a lot of rubbish about duty and civilised values.

He grinned his tangled grin at her, and she told him that it was magical. After she left he studied it in the mirror and decided that she was right. Not that it would do to be complacent.

In the summer they graduated, and were married in what they called a surprise ceremony: a registry office affair with none of their families present, although Rufus had Hector's hefty cheque in his wallet. His mother had hedged when asked if they could honeymoon in Estoril, and so they went to a bed and breakfast in the Lake District.

They did go to Leicester, to visit Rosemary's parents, who had managed to buy their first detached house as war broke out, and had an answer for everything, except their conviction that life had turned against them.

"Bloody socialists," said Mr Richards, "and I don't care if your dad is one of them!"

Then for a few weeks during the Parliamentary recess socialist Dad took his red boxes to the country, and his first shooting party since the war, and Rufus and Rosemary were in the big house in Uppingham Gate. In October Rufus started his job in Manchester, and used Hector's cheque to buy a house in Alderley Edge.

THIRTEEN

Henriwetter they called her, the moment it happened and for some years thereafter. She had been desperate to pee and tugged at Mercy's sleeve but Mercy said "Not now, darling, I'm talking to Miss Hudson."

"But mummy, mummy, mummy …"

"Don't shame me, darling. Be sensible."

"They soon fit in," said Miss Hudson.

"Mummy, mummy ..."

An older girl took Hetty away. Panelled walls leaned in to overpower, landings and dormitories were linoleum-slippery. Hetty turned back to appeal to Mercy, but there was no sign of her. But other girls stared and put out their tongues and that was when her bladder went.

Henriwetters's wearing wet wickers, they chanted thereafter. They boasted about their families. When Hetty talked about hers they said she was stuck up. She was nine, when the oldest girl in the dormitory was twelve.

From the awful moments in which she left Hetty, Mercy drove to London. The winter depressed her. There was no colour in anything. At Uppingham Gate the Fire Service water tanks had been removed but there were still gaps where houses had been bombed. The square's gardens were unkempt but recovering.

"People ask about you," said Hector. "It might be polite to see a few. What d'you say?"

"How could I leave Hetty like that? How do I know it's the right thing?"

Same as ever, thought Hector. She answers one question with another.

"How can we English do such things?" she insisted.

"You did it three times with the boys."

"That was different. I was different."

"And yet you've made the same decision," he said.

She was annoyed and tossed her head.

Perhaps, thought Hector, her decisions have fallen out of step with England. How wild and strange she looks, washed by sun and salt and not caring. She wore a floppy dress that was neither in fashion nor out. Beneath it he discerned the once-responsive body, and wanted to handle it. He felt himself lean towards her but stop. She did not need sex, he realised. She had a purpose beyond it.

Mercy read his thoughts, stabbed them with a glance, and said, "I write to people. All the time. I've had one or two to stay."

"So I heard."

"You never say you'd like to come yourself."

"Wouldn't it risk more hurt than we need?"

It would. Of course it would.

"All sorts of things have happened over there," she said. "We're thinking of opening a shop."

"A shop?"

"Antiques."

"Of course."

"What d'you mean? Why do you say that?"

His apology was gentle.

"A silly joke," he said. "Misplaced."

"A joke?"

"There are three sexes: men, women and antique dealers."

She wanted to be angry but did find it funny.

"So we've known about Malcolm for ever," she said, and thought: my secrets rendered pointless, and what else does he know?

She began to speak, stopped, and re-started.

"Hector, the breadth of your understanding annoys the hell out of me."

"I'm sorry."

"Stop forgiving me. I can't live with it. Haven't you got any awful hidden sins?"

"Of course. D'you want to know them?"

"Yes."

So he told her. She was amazed. She chortled and felt much better. Well, she thought, we have achieved a wonderful something or other. Love, she supposed most people would call it. Next day she returned to Portugal.

*

Hetty, having been taught by Estoril nuns in Portuguese and exasperated fragments of French, was behind in the English curriculum. Her marks were bad and she had no intellectual sense of things: no knowledge of structure or chronology, or of how the world might be ordered.

Neither did she realise how original she was. What she observed seemed obvious to her, but other people were not much interested in it. They followed their fashions or crazes or opinions on which they could all agree. Portuguese became her refuge, in which she talked to herself and imaginary friends.

Girls she did get on with were ones who also lived in odd places, or knew that there was more in the world than England. In time Henriwetters became an affectionate nickname, shortened to Wetters, and people stopped their chants and persecutions. She seemed so floaty, so incapable of the hurt response that bullies crave. Wetters Runacre was a bit boring, was the common wisdom, even when most girls realised that she was not. Yet they could never get close enough to discover more.

Her idea of the holidays was to return to Portugal, but sometimes she had to stay at Uppingham Gate with Hector, and be dumped on friends during the day. Once Rufus and Rosemary were there, and asked questions about Malcolm and her mother, and who was this Federico?

Hetty shrugged and mumbled and Hector rescued her. She hated the unease in the family, and not being able to say things. One day, she knew, someone would ask her to write it all down.

In the meantime, her beach life had made her long-limbed and athletic. She was good at gym and swimming, a leaper at netball and a flowing attacker at hockey, and on a pony she had a sure seat and natural hands. She was lissom and pretty and blonde, as her mother had been.

FOURTEEN

At the General Election of Nineteen Fifty, of which afterwards Hector remembered only his tiredness, the Government's majority was cut to single figures and Hector himself clung to his seat after two recounts.

Then to his surprise he found himself in the Cabinet, when what he wanted was a six month holiday. Colleagues who had been close to great decisions in the War, or heard about them from those who had, were popping pills to keep themselves vibrant, but Hector was prejudiced against drugs and stuck to whisky. Jack Marland, promoted with him, developed an ulcer and could not drink, but was an eager volunteer of hangover remedies; one of them, which he had seen used in the Catalan anarchist militia, involved unscrewing live cartridges and dissolving the powder in water.

"Or," said Jack, "you could always soak gun-cotton."

"What in?" said Hector.

"Hair of the dog?" grinned Jack. "Whisky and water."

It was in the middle of one such conversation, while they waited in the Division lobby, that Hector received a message: go at once to a telephone, where he was told that old Lady Runacre was dead.

If Rufus and Rosemary came to London, he said, he would give them a lift to the funeral. But they had flu and would not move. In the background Rosemary made disparaging remarks about Aneurin Bevan. Then Mercy's flight was delayed by fog and he was left to go alone. The valley was sodden and the village church gloomy. Locals at the graveside were more like rubbernecks than people showing respect, and because the Grange was still unused after the army vacated it, and the Dower

51

House was let, the tea and drinks were in the War Memorial Hall. It smelled of paraffin heaters. He was scrupulous and shook hands but thought: this is the end and I did warn them: but now it won't survive the Death Duties.

Nor did it. Mercy was the Executor of her mother's will and if the solicitor young Hubert Kingly thought that everything had been mishandled, not least by his father old Hubert Kingly, whose mannerisms he maintained plus one or two of his own, he did not say so. "Sell the properties," he advised, "which should give everyone else their legacies and pay off this thieving Government."

On the other side of the desk Hector sniffed, and re-crossed his legs.

"Sorry," said young Hubert. "Slip of the tongue. Oh dear. When d'you fly back, Mercy? Any plans for this evening?"

"A stiff drink at the Savoy," she said, "and then a theatre: something mindless with beautiful clothes."

Later, over her gin and Italian with a cherry on it, she said, "Why do we call him young Hubert when he's sixty if he's a day?"

Hector grinned. My God, he looks tired, she thought. He looks like a clapped-out wolf.

"How do I seem?" she said, to divert him from these thoughts.

"Better," he said. "Let's have a jolly evening."

Which they did. The play was about a life that no longer existed and the actresses wore outfits by Balmain. Then Hector returned to the Commons and Mercy watched from the gallery. At one in the morning they had baked beans on toast at Uppingham Gate, and she slept alone in the room that had been Malcolm's. He was all that mattered now. Her mother was like a historical character, whose death demanded no particular grief.

Ten weeks later an exhausted Labour Government lost the General Election. Hector's seat went with it, as did that of Jack

Marland, which was supposed to be safe. Jack needed money and almost at once took a local job with the Union that had sponsored him. Hector was welcomed back into his old chambers and pondered offers of directorships. Then one day he was asked to visit Clement Attlee in his room at the Palace of Westminster.

"How are you?" said Hector.

The dry little man scraped at his pipe with a match-stick.

"Slugs all over the garden," he said, "but I suppose we mustn't complain."

He tapped down fresh tobacco and tried to light a match.

"You told your constituency party, I gather, that if they so wish they can select a younger man."

"It seems about time," said Hector, thinking: how can someone who sounds like a junior housemaster have achieved so much?

"Very generous," said Attlee. "Very typical of you."

This time the match flared and smoke billowed.

"However," he added, and blew to extinguish the flame, "we still need minds like yours. I've nominated you for a Barony in my Outgoing List."

At school Hetty was summoned by the Head, who announced that from now on she must style herself The Honourable Henrietta Runacre. The Honourable Wettersby, said other girls, not without awe, and in Estoril Malcolm said, "Well, dears, what can we say? Fizzy wine and smugness all round."

FIFTEEN

Four years later London had ceased to smell of dust and cordite and burst gas mains, Magnus was in a military hospital, and on the beach at Estoril Henrietta menstruated for the first time. She was with Malcolm, who said, "Christ, Hetters!" and wrapped a towel round her. Soon that was stained and he said, "I know. We'll walk into the sea." So they stood in the water, he in his trousers, while he wondered what to do next.

He reassured her, shook her hand, and said that now she was a woman, which he wished he could be but never would. Then he remembered something about blood attracting sharks, not that there were any, swept her up and carried her to the villa, where he shouted for help.

Mercy appeared at the top of the stairs, and Federico from the salon that stank of glue and sealants because he used it as a workshop. Mercy's mouth was twisted, as though she wanted to blame Hetty, but all she said was – actually Hetty forgot what she said, because in her mind it became jumbled with later advice from Felicity.

Different from Mercy, yet in her off-handedness not different, Felicity was short and jolly with well-shaped legs, deep breasts, a willing throat and dark hair that tumbled, although as often as not it was piled up in a defiant shambles on top of which she plonked a hat. She had a carrying voice and jolly well knew about things: what pot plants needed food, what sort of vests enabled one's pores to breathe, and what people should do about their problems.

Not that she imposed herself. In fact, as she always said, she was jolly scrupulous not to. But when called upon she was decisive.

Had she not saved the life of Sugden the spaniel, left behind in Mercy's flight to Portugal, when he was run down by a coal lorry? She had, and later, when he was ailing, had his end not been quick and merciful?

"So I don't mollycoddle," she would say. "I tell them: it's only a cold bath, so jump in!"

Her husband had returned from the War a haunted man, who wanted to give up his job in insurance and become a potter. Felicity found him a cottage in Cornwall, installed him, and went back to London, where she lived in what had been her father's rent-protected flat. It overlooked unkempt gardens in Notting Hill and by selling what remained of his possessions she set herself up as an antique dealer.

She had a stall in the Portobello Road and loved the run-down streets, the chatter, the homosexual dealers, the widows who took in lodgers, the workmen's caffs, the Irish and the first of the blacks. Hetty first met her when her father said, "Mrs Hobbs is coming round with a Staffordshire figure I might like."

In fact it was two figures, Sayers and Heenan, the naïve but noble, stripped-to-the-waist opponents in the last bare-knuckle championship fight, of which Hector had an unexpected knowledge from the lurid boys' papers of his youth.

"Who's Mrs Hobbs?" asked Hetty.

"She was a friend of your mother's before the War," said Hector.

Hetty liked her. She was bustly but she did not ask questions, and she was easy to talk to, at a time when Mercy seemed difficult. Hetty wanted to tell her lots, but decided not to when she overheard Mrs Hobbs say out of the side of her lush little mouth, "Does she know about us?"

But she kept that with her other secrets, and was annoyed with herself when on her next birthday visit to Estoril she let slip that she had been to the cinema with Hector and Felicity.

"Felicity?" said her mother. "What Felicity?"

"You know."

"I don't."

"She was your friend."

"What?"

"Mrs Hobbs."

"Oh, *that* Felicity! Her father was regular army. Anglo-Irish. Lost his money at the races. She had to go to work in a milliner's. Sold me my afternoon hats."

"I remember them," said Malcolm, to the rescue as always. "I used to want to try them on."

Hetty felt angry. She hated her family. She wanted to run outside and yell aloud everything she knew. She wanted to scratch her mother's face for being stupid, and to have another existence.

But she could not, and did not know how – until another afternoon and more years later, when John Derker stared at her in the foyer of the Curzon Cinema, Mayfair, and she felt herself go weak between the legs and knew that nothing else mattered.

Within weeks her mother and everyone else except Malcolm was contemptuous of Derker, and Hetty was estranged from them.

SIXTEEN

"What are you doing here?" he had come up to her and said. "Why are you at this film?"

He amazed her. Who was he? He was slobby, and yet how fantastic to be so direct.

"French conversation," she said.

"What?"

"I'm at finishing school."

"You do know it's drivel, don't you?" he said.

"Madame Mercier says it's essential."

"Essential? Madame Mercier? Essential? You're not a bloody Honourable are you?"

"I am," she said. "Yes. As a matter of fact I am."

"Jesus Christ."

"And you're very rude."

He grabbed her wrist and said "Come on!"

"I can't leave my friend."

"You're a red-hot, girl. The Honourable red hot."

And in the crowded foyer he rucked up her dress, kneaded her backside and kissed her.

"Stop it," she struggled. "Stop. Stop it."

"Kiss me again or goodbye," he said, and in the gap she had created by twisting away from him he put his hand over her crutch and she gasped and thought that she would faint.

"Well," he said later when asked if it was true, "it was a rehearsal for the Swinging bloody Sixties, wasn't it?"

When Hector met Derker he deployed a tolerance which he hoped would conceal his disappointment, but Mercy screamed and shouted at Hetty: "This? This lout? How could you?"

"He won a scholarship to Hull and he's going to be a brilliant film director."

"Hull? Hull? Hull's not a university!"

"Of course it's a—"

"He's graceless. He's an oaf."

"No he is not, he's—"

"What? He's what? Energetic? With something new to say? Something worthwhile that we've not heard before?"

There was venom in both of them.

"In the end he'll humiliate you. He's common and cheap and—"

"How can you say that?" screamed Hetty. "How can you say that when we all know what you've done?"

"What I've done? What d'you mean? What have I done?"

Silence. Hetty could not speak. Denial came down like a portcullis.

SEVENTEEN

Should she fear Janet Black? Was John Derker in love with her? These were the questions that came to torment Hetty, not least because in one sense she knew the answers. When commercial television stations opened in Manchester her husband had been attracted by the job advertisements, and so had local girls like Janet, whose confidence and boarding-school education raised her above the secretarial.

She was trained as a vision-mixer, the responsible person who in a studio control room sat next to the director, called out the shot numbers, and pressed the buttons that switched the master-picture from one camera to another, and, using the dissolve and fade levers, could display an artistic sensitivity of her own.

But if Janet was nail-polished efficiency, Hetty was like Mercy without the conviction. A drawl, good manners, insouciance about tidiness, offhand vagueness that expected other people to show a similar decent lack of curiosity – and in her heart fears and confusion, what Johnny called her "emotional anaemia", quoting a poem by Ezra Pound, of whom Hetty had never heard.

She should fuck it and say what she thought, he told her. Be rude. State her claims. Like him.

Johnny's sort were new in the worlds to which he aspired. He had no time to waste. Opportunities were wide open. They trained him as a TV director but what he really wanted was to write. No-one had truly written about England for years, said he and his mates and rivals, but they would. They knew what mattered and after they cracked television they'd crack films. Then watch them. Just watch them and don't get in the way.

To these people, it seemed to Hetty when she met them in after-show pubs, Janet Black was both attractive and well-suited. Hetty had none of their knowledge and found it hard to listen to them. Her mind would wander and she would stare at Janet.

Sexy modern Janet she was called by some, and it was a compliment: clothes that appealed to men, good legs, jokey, laughing when the men laughed. She was not always popular with other girls in the office and studio complex, but not unpopular either; envied because she had the latest in shoes and lipsticks, liked because she would share the news about such things, and did not betray confidences.

In her work she was diligent and not given to panic, and she had her own little car, which her father had insisted on buying because of the studio late nights. She had, after all, to get home to the the Cheshire commuter belt: a big Nineteen Thirties house amid trees, fields rolling away at the back. Her old pony grew fat in the paddock. But that Janet rattled on about such middle-class good fortune seemed to Hetty to be vulgar.

"Bollocks," said Johnny. "It's interesting."

Henrietta demurred.

"Okay. So it's fucking la-di-da. But you know what I mean."

"You fancy her, don't you?" she challenged.

"Everybody fancies her. So what?"

The television people were a city within a provincial city, and had come from all over the place. They went up and down to London, where the ones with theatre backgrounds had friends. In Manchester they knew no-one and did not particularly want to. Wars and decline had dimmed the city's lustre.

Johnny and Hetty started life there in a flat in what had been before the First War a smart suburb, but as Johnny made more money they moved to an old coach-house in Cheshire.

After the children were born it was more difficult for Hetty to go into the city to socialise. Actors and colleagues came out to them, sometimes, but more often Johnny stayed out late to drink and hustle. Then he went freelance and worked in other places, leaving her behind, but he never wanted to talk about moving.

It was never the right time. Just let me get through this run of work. Bastard reviewers. Why don't they know good stuff when they see it?

Hetty half believed him. Hadn't he opened her eyes after a fashion? Why wouldn't he open other people's?

It did not grieve her much that her brother Rufus and Rosemary, although they lived so near, made excuses not to visit, but she was upset that Johnny never went to see his parents. Nothing to say to them. Different worlds, love. I mean, what I write should set them free but do they care? No they don't.

Sometimes Hetty took the children on her own, but it was never enjoyable.

She was tired, when Johnny wanted sexy romance. Paris. Venice. I could winter in Greece or somewhere but you don't see it, do you? He dragged her round museums and battlefields. Every hindrance to their lives had become her fault, somehow.

What she needed was a friend of her own and at first Janet Black had seemed to be the person: flattered, had Hetty but realised, by the interest of someone with a higher claim to social status. They had been on shopping trips, and on same days off Janet took Hetty and the kids out in the car.

Then it stopped, and Hetty knew that it was because Johnny had fucked Janet. She knew it. She knew it and knew it and knew it, so she accused him.

"You're crazy."

"Do you want her and not me?"

"Don't be stupid."

"It's not stupid."

"I haven't fucked her and I don't—"

"Yes you do."

"I don't."

"You do."

He kicked over a chair. The children cried.

"That's your fault. You don't care about them, either."

"I'm here, aren't I? Aren't I? Am I still here or not?"

If what he says is true, she thought, he would be calm. He would soothe and tease and cajole me. He wouldn't shout.

Once she took the children to Portugal but all she could think of was Johnny fucking Janet on the floor of the sitting-room she had left behind. Her mother seemed not to notice her distress, but Malcolm did.

"Want to talk?" he said.

"Not really."

"Gone off me?"

"No."

He looked at her with his head on one side.

"We need something to happen as well," he said. "We're all going potty out here."

He was a joy with the children but Hetty knew what she knew and did not always engage. England was kinder now to homosexuals. If that was the problem they could return.

Then Johnny phoned. Big news. Write and direct. Stars.

"What's it about?" said Hetty, seeing through the open window glittery sea and families under umbrellas. "Is it the Lenin in Zurich idea?"

It was. To her surprise, she was excited.

Back home she said, "Tell me the gossip," expecting something about who the star was having an affair with, and he replied "Janet got married."

"Janet Black?"

"Janet Black."

"Why weren't we invited?"

"That," he said, "is a classic woman's question."

He shook his head. Despite herself she was charmed for an instant and said "Who to?" But she knew the answer, and before he could reply added, "Not that Jeremy person?"

"That Jeremy person."

"Crikey."

"Crikey. And she wore the dress her mother was married in, and her great aunt before that."

"Crikey."

"Invented tradition," said Johnny. "Karl Marx probably had a word for it."

"Jeremy …" mused Hetty.

"Fucking wanker," said Johnny.

Public schoolboy son of a vicar, Second Lieutenant during National Service, played once for the United Services Second Fifteen, Jeremy had gone to drama school but made no subsequent progress as an anyone-for-tennis actor. He was taken on the TV training course but was never more than a floor manager on the news and local chat shows, a seeming subaltern in a corporal's job.

He had a sensitive profile, excellent manners, and a faint smile for the likes of Johnny Derker. Janet's mother thought him ideal for the purpose.

"They bought her a house," added Johnny, "and Janet made a strong opening statement."

"Opening statement?"

"Honeymoon in Capri."

"That's not a statement," said Hetty. "I mean, it might have been in Eighteen Sixty …"

He stared at her. Sometimes she made him feel ignorant.

"Anyway," he persisted, "when she comes back she's moving from Drama to Current Affairs. Associate Producer. World Travel."

"Crikey again!" said Hetty, and thought: I hate her but attagirl! Women can do it! Show 'em, Janet! And attract them, too. Make them all want to fuck you.

She stared at Johnny, and he at her.

What's wrong with me, she thought. My tits? My legs? Stretch marks? Hair? Something I don't realise I'm doing? All he does is stare and say nothing. Yet I want him to succeed, and make money. He can pay, she thought. He can bloody well pay.

EIGHTEEN

Then tectonic plates shifted because on a wet, leaf-blowing night Hector had a seizure. An ambulance came. He was manoeuvred down the Uppingham Gate staircase on a stretcher, and taken to St Stephen's Hospital, where he died two hours later. Mrs Hobbs returned to the house and telephoned Portugal.

Federico answered and there was a lot of shouting and the echoing slaps of slippers on marble. A bleary Mercy came to the phone and Mrs Hobbs said, "I'm telling you first, darling. Then I'll clear out, shall I? Bloody Magnus thinks I'm a she-devil."

She called a taxi, to collect the few clothes and toiletries she kept in the house, and nicked forty pounds from Hector's wallet, leaving twenty. She took as well a seventeeth-century slipware dish that she had always liked and persuaded Hector to buy. She slammed the door behind her, put her keys through the letter-box, and realised that she had left all the lights on. Well, why not, she thought. Everything blazing. A Viking funeral. In the taxi she burst into tears.

Her mind was dry, Mercy realised, as they drank white port and smoked marijuana. It was three in the morning. Winter waves sounded from the shore.

"How d'you feel?" said Malcolm.

"Apprehensive."

They were silent until Federico said "You are Lord Runacre secondo, no?"

"Yes."

"Am I Lady Secundo?"

"Don't be fucking stupid," said Malcolm.

They giggled more when Mercy phoned the hospital and discovered that Hector had been admitted with neither clothes nor possessions beyond a dressing-gown.

"Christ!" said Malcolm. "He died on the job!"

"Well," said Mercy, "Felicity did use the phrase 'in all the circs.'"

"Fantastic way to go," said Malcolm. "What's next?"

They took a dawn walk on the spume-strewn beach, packed, and went to the airport. Mercy phoned the solicitor.

"Hubert," she said. "Don't fart around on your integrity. Just tell me. Good or bad?"

"What I can say," he admonished, "is that you and I are the Executors. Does that satisfy?"

It did.

In twilight they arrived at Uppingham Gate. Mercy's breath tightened when she saw that the lights were on; but she realised what must have happened when she trod on Felicity's keys. Upstairs the bed on which Hector had died was a mess, and there was a fly-swat on the pillow.

"Heavens!" said Malcolm. "He must have used it on Felicity's bottom!"

"Take it all away, darling. Sheets and everything. Put them in the dustbin."

After Portugal the house seemed shabby and out of date. We'll soon see to that, she thought. Then she realised that she still had her coat on, and went downstairs to telephone her other children.

NINETEEN

Hector's funeral was private. Hetty attended but did not like it. She thought that the rest of the family were irritated with her for having made a stupid marriage, and that they had no idea of how upset she was and how close to Hector she had been. She was his favourite, and he had phoned her every week and made secret trips to Manchester, when he would slip her money: just between us, he said.

Mercy was perfunctory and seemed to want the matter to be over. She was impatient with Hetty's children. "Aren't they a bit young for a funeral, darling? Do they have any idea what it means?"

Nor would she say what her own plans were. Stay in England or return to Estoril? Too early to say, darling, and anyway – and anyway, Malcolm was not at the funeral, having got the flu, and deciding not to pass it on.

Rosemary was almost openly rude about this, and grumbled in a corner with Magnus. Hit in the spine by a guerilla's bullet in Malaya, he was walking again, if on a stick, and unsure of his future. His voice boomed but he seemed pre-occupied by something far away, that he had seen but could not understand. He had taken it upon himself to liaise on the family's behalf with legal and political colleagues who would organise a memorial service for Hector at St Margaret's Westminster.

Hetty decided not to attend it, whenever or wherever it was, and went home.

Derker was in Hollywood. After the success of Lenin in Zurich he urged his agent to push hard for America and was shirty when nothing happened. His agent took him to lunch and said "What's your power base? It's your trendy lefties like yourself."

"Trendy lefties?"

"Stay with them. The Yanks don't want to know."

Derker tipped his bowl of spaghetti into the agent's lap and walked out.

The agent borrowed a pair of chef's checked trousers from the kitchen, returned to his office and was told that an obscure producer in Los Angeles had just phoned with an enquiry about John Derker. For the moment rage was swallowed.

Two days later John Derker phoned to say that he was sorry but he could get het up over political principles and actually – and actually, lied the agent, I was about to tell you what I had pulled off on your behalf.

So the spaghetti incident became a comic legend among certain people, and Derker was sent with his showreel to a Los Angeles motel. He phoned sometimes and pretended to be interested in Hetty's news.

Her mother was still in England and seemed to be more interested in the grandchildren but always phoned when it was difficult for Hetty. The din. The imminent school run. Someone at the door who needed to be paid. Oh. And in Hector's will he left me a painting.

"Worth anything?"

She'd no idea. Victorian. A knight and a lady in a forest.

"Jesus Christ," said Derker. "Can't you find out?"

Typical, she thought, and did not remind him of what the painting meant to her: its image had inspired Malcolm to invent their faery kingdom of Autumnia.

Three days later Derker was home, having argued with the American producer and failed to interest anyone else. But he was agitated by something more.

"What is it? What's wrong?"

"Don't ask."

"What have I done? Is it me?"

"Don't."

But she was a more confident woman now, and she persisted.

"Okay," he said. "It's Janet."

"Janet?"

"Janet Black."

"You mean you met her in America?"

"She's dead."

"What?"

"Dead."

"How? Why?"

"Helicopter."

"What?"

"Oh come on. You must have seen it on the news. Don't you watch the news? It was everywhere, all over the world."

"What was? You know I never watch the news."

An American news crew helicopter had failed in mid-air and crashed into a Guatemalan shanty-town. The cameraman kept filming. The sky tilted and the ground rushed out of focus. People screamed. Blackout.

"She was aboard?"

"Aboard. She was. I don't know what to do anymore."

TWENTY

Resentment grew over time, as they all watched what happened at Uppingham Gate. An opium den, Magnus called it, a sort of fake oriental male brothel with perfumed candles, cushions on the floor, sound systems everywhere. Its main spaces were showrooms for antiques that came and went, a business pursued with vigour, and clients wooed at parties that were word of mouth wonders in the new London.

Swinging London, that is. No longer peeling, damage-smelling, bomb pocked London, or disrespectful, intense, creative Fifties London, but mini-skirt London. Birth control and fuck without risk London. But do they, wondered Mercy. Despite everything, do many people really do it as casually as I used to eat glacé fruits? And where will it lead in the end?

Young men came to the parties with long hair like cavaliers.

Some of them wore antique military jackets over jeans, scarlet and gold, about which Mercy had a qualm. Had not officers died in such coats?

Now people mocked what they had died for, and quite decent girls thought that Cockney hustlers were more interesting, although to Mercy it was what she thought she had stood for, and why the War was fought. But there is exhilaration, she persuaded herself. I'm part of something. My son needs me to be part of something: the freedom of the young, and their journey to brighter places.

"You surely understand," she said to Hetty on the phone. "You're a mother yourself. You do understand, don't you?"

TWENTY-ONE

It was Rosemary who put an end to it, rather as later the Arabs raised the price of oil and London no longer swung. It's all lies, she said. Lies, lies, lies, year after year. We've all been forced to live a lie.

Rufus protested. Who was forced? Nobody.

"She'd have gone mad," he said. "If Malcolm hadn't come home it would have deranged her."

"No it wouldn't."

"Her view of herself. Everyone else's view of her. What Father thought and—"

"Oh, your father loved her. I'll give him that."

"We all love her."

"Love's blind. In this case worse than blind."

Her essential point he could not deny, and as one cotton mill after another closed and it was clear that the hundred-year-old business would have to be wound up, he knew that his life must change anyway. Rosemary had already started a white goods

68

business, dealing with the very Asian manufacturers whose prices had destroyed them.

Then she astounded him by suggesting that they make up with Hetty and use her as a salesperson.

"You can't do that. She's painfully timid."

"Nonsense. Once off the hook she'll be a tigress."

Which proved to be the case.

She had already slipped the hook, when it was discovered that Janet Black's death was a false rumour. She told Derker to leave and jumped at the chance of working. Derker complained, was dumped by a younger girlfriend, and made TV commercials, which he called films. So who was Rufus to argue?

Rosemary made him feel like a man, when Mercy always made him feel a cripple. Or so he told himself. And there was Magnus, sour beyond his years, unhappy because he could not find a wife, when it was his unhappiness that put them off.

In the court case that overturned everything the decisive, or at least the most sensational evidence was that of Group Captain Vesey, who held a senior post in procurement at the Air Ministry, and had at first refused to appear. But a subpoena would look bad, the Service decided, and German TV and newspapers were already aware. Indeed, they had been sniffing in vain for some time, which is how through an old chum in Berlin Magnus came to hear, and told Rosemary that it was now or never.

Counsel understood Vesey's feelings and dealt with them at the outset.

"You had an early opportunity, I believe, to apprise the late Lord Runacre of what you will tell the Court today?"

"I did."

"Why didn't you take it?"

"Lost my nerve."

"How so?"

"No wish to inflict pain. No useful purpose. Why do it."

A silence. Counsel looked at His Lordship, who gave the tiniest signal.

Point taken.

Proceed.

"You had no idea then, of course, of what would subsequently happen within the Runacre family?"

"None."

Most of them were in Court, and Vesey had avoided their eyes.

As a junior, Counsel had known Lord Runacre, and liked him, and in his opinion this case which could only end in humiliation should never have come to Court.

Why would anyone shove in their mother's face the witnesses he had yet to call, who would talk about aircrews using drink and drugs, and the desperate if improper love between Malcolm and a batman? Why would a mother deny everything? Had she misread Vesey? Or did she actually believe what could never have been true?

Counsel took a breath and came at once, and mercifully he hoped, to the shooting down of the Lancaster.

"Pilot Officer Runacre was deceived by scarecrow flares. I tried to tell him but he wouldn't listen."

Actually Vesey hadn't wanted to say that, and stopped.

Counsel waited.

"We bailed out. Thrown out, really. My chute opened. I landed in a farmyard. It was chaos. Half the aircraft had fallen on the village, you see. Burning aviation spirit. People were killed. Others were very angry."

"They threatened you?"

"Two German soldiers on leave protected me."

"Then what happened?"

"Pilot Officer Runacre appeared."

"Appeared?"

"Yes. Well. He came down the road. He was bleeding. I don't suppose he knew where he was. Not properly, anyway. And then—"

Silence. Counsel waited. Vesey tried to speak but it dried in his throat. Counsel gestured at the glass of water.

"Thank you," said Vesey, and sipped.

"Anyway," he continued, in a rapid voice to be sure to get through it. "Before anyone could do anything one of the villagers ran at Runacre and stabbed him with a pitchfork. Then someone else – Anyway. They killed him."

A woman wailed in agony. Mercy? Maybe. Someone else knocked over a pile of law books. His Lordship held up a hand and there was order.

"Why didn't they kill you?" said Counsel.

"Ashamed, I suppose. And one of the soldiers had a weapon."

"What did they do with Runacre's body?"

"Military vehicles arrived. One of them took me away."

"Pilot Officer Runacre …"

"I think – Well. Matter of fact, the soldiers did a deal. Keep me alive. Throw the body to the pigs. Say nothing."

Staff were called because the woman hyperventilated. Reporters sent copy-boys to the phones. His Lordship knocked with his gavel.

Counsel re-commenced with a look around the entire courtroom.

"Was Pilot Officer Runacre friendly with a batman?"

"Yes."

"Did you know him?"

"Slightly."

"What was his name?"

"Slater. Aircraftman Slater. Charlie Slater."

Counsel sighed and nodded.

"They looked a bit alike, actually," said Vesey.

"Please concentrate. Tell me. Do you see this Mr Slater in the Courtroom?"

"Yes."

"Where?"

Vesey breathed, twisted his lips, looked up, and said "There," as he pointed to Malcolm, Lord Runacre.

*

Jack Marland had been called out to reassure his union members who worked there that when the Alder Mill was shut down in two weeks' time they would receive the agreed redundancy pay.

When as he left he looked into the office the Mill Secretary said "Have a cup of tea," and so they sat on high stools at the built-in Victorian desk that overlooked the mill yard: the spring sunshine, the weeds and fluffs of cotton waste between the cobbles, the bulk of the mill, its hoist doors open, the whine of machinery and to one side the old sheds, the coal heaps and trees with new green on them.

The Secretary was a weedy sort of man but he managed a smile.

"What will you do?" said Jack.

"Try and get a Sub Post Office," said the Secretary.

They considered it. The world that they had known since they were born was seeping away, which in the midst of so much, seeming prosperity confused them.

Then Jack saw the headlines across the Secretary's morning paper.

Impersonation. Homosexuality. Courtroom scenes. The Runacre scandal.

He could not help himself.

"Well," he said in a dead voice, as though it was the end, "I'll get off at Edgehill."

"You'll what?"

Jack explained. Edgehill is the last station before the Lime Street terminus. Getting off there is Liverpool slang for coitus interruptus.

"Right," said the Secretary. "Right. But how does it apply in this case?"

"Oh it doesn't," said Jack. "We just used it to mean anything, really. I suppose it meant we didn't have to think."

Art Movers

Charlie March was called March because that was the month of his birth, when as soon as he was wiped clean of mucus and wrapped he was taken from his mother to the orphanage. He was not curious about this, and had no sense of deprivation; or so it seemed for many years. He had been four when he was fostered by Mr Macauley and his younger wife. Mr Macauley was the son of a loom overlooker, but had won a scholarship to the Grammar School and after Hitler's war and Teacher Training College returned as History master.

A Victorian foundation with an asphalt yard, the school had farmland and between-wars ribbon development behind, and in front the Pennine spur on which the town was built: the hulks of the cotton mills, the terraces and waste ground and spiky chapels: a panorama wreathed in smoke that made it seem romantic, but by the 1960s was revealed by Clean Air Acts to be raddled and exhausted.

Not that people cared. They were blithe and had money to spend, even as the mills closed, and Mr Macauley's attitude to this was seen as evidence of how out-of-date he was; and as the Government made the Grammar a Comprehensive, and the Council built over the playing field, his criticisms of the curriculum were deemed incorrect, and he was eased into administration.

His way of judging people, inherited from a world that was dying before he was born, did not alter. He reckoned that Charlie was a practical sort of person, and steered him towards technical courses; from which Charlie joined the Royal Engineers and was an ideal soldier.

He had learned young how to live in an institution and Mrs Macauley, shrewd but gentle, had encouraged his habits of observation and helpfulness, so that his reliability was never boastful.

Mr Macauley was a stickler for tidy haircuts, clean shoes and not dropping litter, and he liked his pipe, the bowling green and Gilbert and Sullivan. He had kept his hard-earned schoolboy books and prizes and they were devoured by Charlie: the atlas with a quarter of the globe coloured red, the adventure stories, the poems that were once in every classroom anthology. Take my drum to England, hang it by the shore, beat it when your powder's running low.

Mr Macauley would also tell Charlie how he had been encouraged by a teacher named Miss Ogden. Her fiancé had been killed at Ypres. His name was on the Menin Gate, and for years Miss Ogden would go there each summer, to hear the bugle sound the Last Post.

So if many of the men Charlie knew in the army were there because they could find nowhere else to go, to him its ideals seemed as natural as your Rock and Roll. He understood what it had meant to be in the thin red line at Waterloo, to face your front and fire at the young gentleman's command. It kept the world safe and someone had to do it.

In the Falklands he removed, so that mines could be cleared, Argentinian corpses that came to mush in his gloves; in the Iraq desert signals went wrong, their own planes blasted them, and his mate's head was blown off; in sullen Ulster and Afghanistan he thought that some places were as they were and did not want to change, perhaps, not in their ancient depths.

Then at home nobody cared what he'd done. It embarrassed them. They stared at him but did not see him, and heroes were no longer men who protected your body with theirs when you were wounded, but singers in boy bands who wore mascara and tight trousers.

Even the youths Charlie employed years later had dismissive smirks if they sussed that he had been in the army – or so it seemed when he felt at odds with himself, which he tried to allow not to happen. He had intended to sign on for fifteen more years, but did not see the point, somehow.

He went home, where Mr Macauley was dead and the mills and half the town pulled down, and when he passed veiled mothers in the street it was Helmand again, and were there explosives in the pushchair? Then he dreamed that there were and he was blown up outside a discount store.

He awoke yelling, and Mrs Macauley made them tea.

"It'll be fine," she said. "You go. There's nothing here anymore. There'd be nothing for me if I was your age."

Charlie wanted work as a mechanic and went to London to look up an old oppo named China Johnson. China was married and lived in a council house in Acton. Charlie slept on the downstairs sofa, which at first Mrs China didn't like; then she realised that Charlie had cleaned the fireplace and done half the chores before she woke up, and saw the point of him. She asked him to stay another month, during which chance intervened.

China worked for a firm of removers, and three or four blokes were off sick in a flu epidemic. China suggested to his chief packer that Charlie go in as a temp. Charlie did and enjoyed himself: the furniture manoeuvring, the jokes in the cab, the driving around, the people they met. After ten days he saw his opportunity.

They moved a widow from a house to a small flat, and on the morning of the second day took her surplus furniture and pictures to an auction house: a world of officers and chancers and would-be gentlemen, Charlie realised. He knew at once how to deal with it, and was interested in pictures because Mr Macauley used to take him to Manchester City Art Gallery. They argued about Picasso, none of whose works they had seen, but who Mr Macauley believed to have contributed to the emergence of what he called "such cavemen as your Rolling Stones."

West End auction houses and the high level dealers had contracts with big shippers, but everyone else, from smart galleries to weekend stallholders at Portobello, needed stuff to be moved around, and Charlie had enough money saved to buy a second-hand Transit, fix it up with racks and webbing and buy insurance cover. He was in business, square and grizzled, in his uniform of sleeveless fleece, work shorts and boots with rolled-down socks. He found his own place in Hammersmith and fell into an affair with

Beth, who dealt in French country furniture and lived above her shop, so that one day a decade and a half later –

"Anything else?" he said, knowing that there was, and she said "Yes. I've thought it through. I want you to either move in for good or go away and we split."

"Is that a proposal of marriage?"

"Not exactly."

Hair up but untidy, tall, warm, intense, nothing under the caftan, she looked marvellous. Charlie wanted to grab her but felt hollow. "So?" said her stare.

"Right," he said, dry-throated, and went to the van. Carlos was on headphones. Tommo half-guessed the situation and had a foolish grin.

"What?" said Charlie.

"Nothing."

"Say something helpful and I'll knock your block off."

"Right," said Tommo, and thought: this is not the moment.

They delivered Beth's armoire to the restorer in Lots Road and the Garden Centre was nearby. They loaded up and Tommo swallowed and said "My zipper. Remember? It's on the way. Can we?"

At the dry cleaners opposite the station Delivery Ali arrived early, clothes on hangers brought in, and the bags of stuff to go taken out.

"What's this?" said Cindy. "First time in two years you're not late?"

"One of them days, innit?" he replied, and thought: fat white slag, why don't they sack her?

Because she worked here on and off before we bought it, they told him, and she knows the routines and the customers.

Ali swerved out, stamping to show the crusader bitch that he despised her. When he was gone her mobile rang.

What she heard knocked everything out of her. She slid down the wall and held the phone so hard that her thumb hurt.

The van stopped outside and Tommo came in and said "Oh!" because nobody was there.

Cindy clambered up, tears shiny and mouth open.

"Are you okay?" said Tommo.

"What?"

"Okay."

"Can you come back tomorrow?" said Cindy.

"Sure," he said, but did not move.

"I'm fine," said Cindy. "I've just got to close the shop."

Tommo decided that nothing he said would make a difference, and left.

Cindy secured the yard door, grabbed her coat and handbag, scrawled SORRY EMERGENCY PHONE CALL on the CLOSED notice, and ran across the road to the station.

"What's happening?" said Charlie. "Where's she going?"

"Emergency Phone Call," read Carlos.

"And we've had a few of those," said Charlie.

"It's my lottery ticket," said Tommo. "I think I've won. It's in the pocket."

"Pocket?"

"Of my zipper. That's in the cleaners."

Further on, in Dulwich Village, they carried the load round the side of the house: a dozen box balls in plastic tubs, and statuary: two urns and a stone greyhound.

"How Charlie come to gardens now?" Carlos wanted to know.

"Favour for a friend."

"Who?"

"Fat Percy," said Tommo. "You know."

"Okay."

There was soil in the empty van, and Carlos swept it out.

Cindy bailed out of the Tube and took a taxi. Money, she thought. Trev'll go bananas about the money.

Charlie was in what Tommo called his Helmand Province Mood: brisk despite the incoming. "Sausage sandwiches," he said. "Next greasy spoon. I've time before I drop you lot and pick up again."

Outside the hospital there were smokers, and butts all over the pavement. Cindy was at the Main Entrance instead of A and E. Someone helped her but it was too late. Her mother had died on the trolley minutes after admittance.

"Si," said Carlos. He was from Bogota and studying chemistry at Imperial College. He liked the out-of-term cash. "Sure. I do tomorrow. Okay."

"But you can't, can you?" said Charlie, slurping ketchup.

"I'm okay for Friday, though," said Tommo. "Why don't I text Richie for tomorrow?"

"I worry about Richie," said Charlie.

Tommo's zipper was in this particular dry cleaners because his Art College was nearby, and SORRY EMERGENCY PHONE CALL was still on the door. Tommo rattled it and looked around. Someone in the Health Café gave him a shrug and head shake. Tommo thought: this is only worth it if I actually have won the Lottery.

In the Knightsbridge Estate Agency of Willoughby and Lamont, Harry's mobile pinged and the message was a selfie of a woman's crotch and at first he thought it was Annabel's but then he realised it was Lucy's (same pubic hair, that curious non-colour that hides the vaginas of blondes) and he had an erection and at the same time saw that old Willoughby was staring at it across the office, so he sat down. Then the desk phone rang and it was his client from Belarus with more queries about the penthouse in Rutland Gate.

"No formal offer so far," said Harry. "I think we should hold our nerve."

Then pretending for Willoughby's sake to be writing notes behind the up-tipped computer screens he texted with one finger the instructions to Lucy. Tomorrow. Time and place. Suspender belt. How she got off from school was her business.

Charlie's afternoon pick-up was the latest in a series of jobs that he had fallen into when he moved a Ruhlmann sofa and chairs into an Eaton Square first floor. The owner was a lawyer who had weighed Charlie's military composure and said "Some deliveries are no questions asked, I suppose?"

"Are they?" said Charlie.

"Occasional ones for me could be."

It was in the early days with Beth and she said "Cocaine. Don't touch it."

But Charlie knew the difference between criminal and discreet, and the lawyer was a woman.

From where he dropped Carlos it took an hour in heavy traffic to Islington: a leafy square, a low Council block on the side that had been blitzed, a Queen Anne brick terrace on the other. Handy for the City, he thought, and double-parked.

An elegant wisp of a twenty-year old opened the door.

"I'm from the lawyer," he said.

"Mr March?"

"Yes."

"Golly."

She was pregnant, he realised, as she turned to pick up the carrier. He checked what was in it: a Lowry, the sort of scene that was in Charlie's blood: tiers of windows in a mill, its chimney, a corner shop.

It was wrapped in a single fold of bubble. Shows how little he cares, thought Charlie, and said "All correct. Thank you."

She hesitated.

"You've not met her, have you? I mean, is she really an alcoholic?"

"I've met you," he smiled, "and you've been very helpful."

Blocked motorists banged on their horns. Get back to your bloody van.

London, he thought. I remember when it wasn't like this, and when it didn't take another hour to get from Islington to – he was halfway there when a text said that the lawyer's client couldn't wait. She'd gone to the salon. Meet her there.

He found a space in Belgrave Square and walked. There were black girl receptionists, humming blowdryers, male cutters with their sleeves rolled to mid-forearm, windows at back and front, the scents of oils and shampoos. The receptionist eyed him over and said "She's there. With Alesha."

Alesha was Indian and voluble and Charlie said "Alesha? A delivery for your client."

Alesha had the colouring paste and silver foil, and the client a pot of tea and an éclair, which she ate with one hand while a manicurist crouched over the other.

Rings, observed Charlie. A big stone and a Cartier. Ho hum.

He held up the bag. She nodded. Put it there.

"I suppose you didn't see the bastard himself?" she said.

"It was just a pick-up," said Charlie.

She tried to smile.

A good-looker thirty years ago, he thought, and on the return to the van: smart: no Lowry declared to the Court, so the lawyer can go easy somewhere else. And Mr Macauley's story about passing Lowry on Tib Lane, Manchester.

"Afternoon, Mr Lowry," said Mr Macauley, and Lowry said "Afternoon."

Afterwards Mr Macauley wasn't sure that it had been Lowry, but it must have been, thought Charlie. Mustn't it?

His reaction to Beth's ultimatum had been awkwardness as though everyone was staring at him. Then anger. Then feeling stupid. Then – she's your posh totty, Jack Shade had grinned, and you're her rough trade. Lucky both. Was that it, then? Charlie pleased with himself and she with herself? Meeting when the urge was on one or the other and not too many questions? Had he described his worst dreams? Never. She hadn't wanted to know. But he had woken up shouting. At which she held him. It's okay. We're together. I won't ask and don't you ask me. Of course she had told about her smart childhood and some of the other men. She said very comical things about them. And there's the one she still sees. He took her on a weekend. Monaco Grand Prix. And her daughter's in Brighton. Had her when she was seventeen. And the friends who think that Charlie's uncouth and—

Why now? What had happened? Why was she dumping him? What did she want? Why? What had he done differently or wrong? Was he himself different, and had she detected it? He still wanted her. The sex was still – But could it be with anyone? Had she decided this? What did she want him to admit? Could he – The question he avoided. The one he never wanted to hear. Could he hold it together without her? Not allow drink or drugs to wipe everything away, not betray, not be like Shade but still hold together. Work hard. Jobs properly done. Keep good order. Thin red line. Man standing next to him blown to shreds. He did not want that memory to be in the room with her. He talked aloud to himself. Each task. Hoover. Iron two shirts. Cook. Wash up. Think about tomorrow. Work calls. He dialled. Rufus couldn't do it. Ahmed's phone whined and cut out. The Chilean friend of Carlos was on answer. He called Richie.

"Yeah," said Richie, "Tommo texted me. I can do it."

A and E was crowded all night and Cindy wasn't discovered until morning. She had found excuses and hiding places and decided not to leave until she knew how to change her life. How to vanish and come back as someone else. Then the staff caught up with her and said "She's traumatised. She should stay." Meanwhile Trev was non-plussed and the owners of the shop discovered that it had been closed all day.

They were shown the pictures under consideration and went outside for a cigarette. "Jesus," said Richie, "I could do better than that in my sleep."

"Good," said Charlie. "Bring it in Monday morning."

'That' was a late Terry Frost. Very colourful. Five figures at auction.

"But what's it about?" said Richie. "Where's the relevance?"

Carlos, who remembered his uncle kidnapped by para-militaries, an ear cut off and sent by post as proof of life, thought that most English indignation was ridiculous. So he said nothing.

Richie smirked. He was nineteen and knew everything.

Eleanor from the Estate Agency arrived in her open-top Mini. Her park blocked the van's exit, but we'll sort that out later, thought Charlie. The yard had once served the Wandsworth Matting Factory, announced faded Edwardian paintwork.

Young Peter came out of the storage. His suit had very narrow trousers.

"Hi, Eleanor," he said. "Super necklace."

"Oh, d'you think so?"

"When you've made your pick there's the boring insurance paperwork."

When Tommo came down from the Calder Valley he had looked in a newsagent's window and found a room in a council flat but now the man had a new girlfriend and she didn't like Tommo and had asked him to leave. So he had gone online and found a place even nearer College. But the woman wanted to meet people before deciding. On his way to see her he tried the dry-cleaners again but it was still closed.

The show apartment was on the twentieth floor of a glittery new South of the River development. It had views of the other towers, and then south. Barely an actual river glimpse.

"We're joint agents with Willoughby's but they're foot-dragging," said Eleanor. "So we've decided to go ahead and tell them afterwards."

That was, to dress the flat, hang serious pictures in it, and include the buyer's choice of one of them in the final price. It had worked a treat in Vauxhall, she said. It offered a lifestyle.

"I remember," said Charlie, wielding his measure to be sure that the pictures would fit the lift, which opened into the apartment.

When it did so there were cries and gasps and a girl wearing a suspender belt and black stockings pummelled the floor as she was entered from behind by a tousle-haired young man who was naked but for one red and yellow sock.

"Harry?"

"…?"

The girl yelled and ran off. Harry flopped off balance, recovered, hand over dwindling penis, and said "Charlie?"

"I could have been with a client!" hissed Eleanor.

Ceiling's a bit low, thought Charlie, and the other blocks a bit too near. Developer greed.

"Mayday," he said. "You've seven minutes to get out. Be aware that my lads are at the service ramp."

"Is it your knowledge of the case," said the Charge Nurse, "that Cindy's been prescribed Diazepam but still buys other—"

"Diaza what?" said Trev.

"It's for anxiety."

"Headache pills. If we get hangovers she takes headache pills."

"What sort?"

Search me. Search me why it was one mess after another that he had to sort out, such as yesterday, the kids come from school but nobody at home and no bloody idea of what had happened.

"Friday night," he said. "I take a drink Friday night."

The Charge Nurse had heard it before.

And as for her bloody mother being dead, that no-one told me she was just goes to prove what—

"Does she drink on her own?" said the Charge Nurse. "And would you know if she does?"

Charlie paid the boys ten pounds an hour cash for moving work, but picture-hanging like this earned more: fifteen if they were with him, but twenty if he sent them out on their own, or if someone asked them to do it on the side. This, he reckoned, was a reflection of the British class system. Muscle was cheap but hanging required judgement, and was a superior activity.

Trev held Cindy's hand and said "The kids are devastated. They're all over the place. And I'll do better. I promise. I'll do better." Thinking: what's better? I work like buggery as it is. Cindy sniffed and said "I think they've injected me with something."

Carlos held one end of a vivid blue and orange Albert Irwin and Richie held the other and sang "We still love Jeremy Corbyn …" sotto voce.

Eleanor couldn't decide. More to the left. No. Back again.

Outside there was the noise of a helicopter. Charlie remembered the one he'd prayed for, and the girl medic who jumped out, helmet jammed over her pony-tail.

"One, two, now!" she ordered, and Charlie took his hand off the wound pad. She wrapped a dressing over it as quick as you please, and Charlie rolled away to return fire.

"What d'you think?"

"What?"

The officer's blood had soaked Charlie's uniform.

"Oh – Er—"

He gestured. A tad up. Okay. He made the pencil marks. The boys lifted the picture away and to test Carlos he said "So where do we drill?" and Carlos said where and Charlie said "Good lad!", knowing that he could send him out on his own.

Eleanor made a face. She was a big woman, angular and no nonsense. Would she complain about that daft Harry they'd caught fucking, or be lenient?

Jack Shade woke up, thought he'd pissed himself, realised that he hadn't but needed to, and sat on the lavatory. He still wore his shirt and hadn't removed his watch. He had sweated and stank. He wiped himself, stood, and felt dizzy. His temples ached and his hands tingled and seemed unable to grip. If he held the basin his fingers might slide off, he thought, so he clutched the taps and looked in the mirror. His eyes were still the blue of ice and courage, but a tooth was chipped and there were broken veins. Security, he knew, was not to be there when it happened, and he wasn't there, he was in Manchester in an Airbnb in a tower block with a panoramic view of what the Nineteenth Century and Britain's greatness had left behind, and all he had with him were his hangover, two pay-phones, empty bottles and anxiety. He should ring the office, he supposed. But did they care? Had they already sussed that he had crossed the line? He ran the shower lukewarm and the wet shirt stuck to him and the watch was waterproof at sixty metres or whatever, and it's a rat-fucked world, he thought. Nobody does anything properly anymore, they all think that they can have whatever they want whenever they want it, so the drink's a sort of means test: how far can you go until your body says enough, you're dead?

Mrs Buggy opened the door and Tommo said "Oh!" because she was wearing a man's pyjamas and dressing-gown.

"I'm on nights," she said, "but don't think it means that you can bring girls in."

"You mean I've got the room?"

"Not yet," she said, thinking: his eyes are bright, he's properly shaved and he's nervous but cheeky at the same time, which makes me laugh, actually.

In the kitchen she said "How many sugars?"

It's a bit dusty, he thought and there are things everywhere.

She read his glance.

"My late husband. Always buying things to mend. Then he upped and died."

"Downed and died," said Tommo. "Sorry."

She was full-bodied, Irish, and about his mother's age.

And it was two minutes from College, and perfect.

"The last one brought in oil paints," she said. "But I won't have that. So I fired him."

"I've a studio space."

"So did he."

But she'd take him on probation, she said, and explained that there were Asians next door. Three kids. Very polite. Three doors down a portaloo and the builders. Poshification or whatever it's called, bugger us all.

Carlos had bought a salad box and ate as they drove the spare pictures back to the storage. Richie muttered and jerked his body. Carlos looked and Richie said "Stop your problem, man. I'm rehearsing."

"Rehearsing?"

"Stand-up. It's more immediate."

Carlos did not chew for a moment and Charlie said "Still in the garage?"

Richie's parents had a pebble-dashed suburban semi and Richie had moved out of the house and into the garage because he couldn't stand his sister and needed the space; and anyway, it was their fault he'd been fired from art college.

"I've put up inside cladding," he said. "Bigger speakers. They can't hear a fucking thing."

But his mother would still bring his meals across.

Trev was a vehicle delivery driver and had already missed one day's work and didn't know how he could carry on without Cindy because of the overnights. He was scared. He ransacked her clothes boxes and found three bottles of cider, and empties in the bins outside the flats. The kitchen was a mess, stuff piled up in the sink. He met the kids from school and took them to McDonald's.

"When will we see her? What's happening? We want her."

He phoned Cindy's sister who said "Get lost. It was all your fault in the first place," and hung up. The kids stared at him.

There was something else that in order to function Charlie tried to push away, something that he had noticed when Beth thought that he wasn't in the room. All day, despite his best efforts not to, he saw it again and in the evening phoned her.

"I'm just ringing to say that I'm not ready to ring yet."

"No."

Her voice had no energy.

"Are you okay?"

Deliberate brightness.

"Of course."

"I've got another Fat Percy gig tomorrow."

"Give him my love."

"Yes."

"Hang on a minute," she said. "Water's boiling."

"I'll go."

"No."

She laid the phone down. He heard voices.

Was she older than him? He supposed she was. Maybe. He'd never insisted, and on birthdays she always counted backwards from thirty-nine.

More noises. He looked around. His flat was shiny clean but empty, almost.

"Charlie?"

"Yes."

"Soon, though. It has to be soon."

"Yes."

She hung up.

"It's what the whole thing's about," said Fat Percy. "Illuminating lives. Spiritual values passed on."

He tugged the silk handkerchief from his breast pocket, blew his nose, and dabbed at his eyes.

"The utter shock when a painting speaks to us," he continued. "So forget rent rises. Forget fucking business rates and the entire auction house hypocrisy scam, even ..."

He raised his spectacles on their neck cord to observe Charlie more clearly.

"Even the utter collapse and perversion of the art world ..."

He blew his nose again, threw the rumpled silk into the waste paper basket and said "Fetch us another one, Adrian, there's a good soldier ..."

Adrian had removed his jacket to assist Charlie in wrapping, and his braces were resplendent. He brought another silk square from the stack in the desk cupboard, which also contained Japanese whisky and the shot glasses.

"By perversion I mean that in my father's day there was connoisseurship, but what most people buy art for today is a profit …"

Charlie said nothing. Percy's father, he knew, had been a retail chemist in Surbiton, who hated what he called namby-pambys in the art world, and when Charlie became an auction-house porter would not speak to him for seven years.

"Unfortunately," concluded Percy, "I blame Gauguin and Van Gogh."

"Van Gogh?"

"The ignored geniuses who turned out to be worth millions. That's what did it. The idea that the avant-garde pays off. Like the money market. But will it always? Have you looked at today's supposed avant-garde? More dumbed down celebrity rubbish. So is he famous because he sculpts, or because he wears a frock?"

He's not actually fat, thought Charlie, but portly in a way that adds conviction to what he says.

"Right," said Adrian, on his knees to unroll more bubble-wrap. "Pass me the Sickert."

It was a Camden Town interior: a woman dressing: careless, but intense in the moment. Percy held it out in one hand.

"Sorry to see it go, really," he said. "In the old Fulham flat it was on the back of my wardrobe door. I could tie my tie and study it."

Charlie and Beth had discussed Percy many times. If he had a weakness it was that at heart he wasn't a dealer but a collector. So he paid too much and rising overheads were a worry.

Not that the second divorce had improved matters, opined Beth.

Charlie's phone went: the lads in the van.

"Right," said Charlie, and to explain: "We're on a double yellow."

"There you are," said Percy. "Another instance. Preposterous mini-cabs and cyclists."

There were construction works: offices being converted into flats at three million each, scaffolding, wooden partitions over the pavement, a power crane blocking one lane: the van's drive round the block took ten minutes.

But there was an illegal space outside the gallery.

"Drone missile it," said Carlos. "What the hell?"

Trev went to the hospital but Cindy had already been discharged, they said, and gone home in a taxi. He returned. She wasn't there.

It was a small mansion block in what Percy called one of those nowhere districts north of Kensal Green. The lift had been installed later and was small, so they juggled the larger painting through the shabby common parts and up the stairs.

The man at the door wore a cardigan over a shirt and tie and Adrian said "Mr Ransome? Gallery de Freitas. We've brought your bonbons."

Mr Ransome said "Adrian, isn't it, if I remember rightly? We're in the end room."

Charlie knew the atmosphere at once: the reproductions on the corridor wall, the books, the furniture that had been the best they could afford, the careful lives: Mr and Mrs Macauley.

The bay window had a surprising view, in the distance of which specks of planes queued up for Heathrow, and Mrs Ransome's walking stick was tucked beside her in the armchair. She had a luminous smile, but her clothes had become too big, and her face was chalky.

"Unwrap?" said Adrian. "Hang? Take away the bubble? What d'you think?"

"Cup of tea," said Mrs Ransome. "We bought a carrot cake."

The paintings smouldered. They were breath-taking. Percy's eye, thought Charlie.

When they climbed back into the van they sat in silence. Then Charlie looked and Adrian said "I don't know. We didn't ask."

Charlie started the van. Maybe fifty thousand, he thought. A good hit for Percy. And Mrs Ransome, a woman dying if ever he saw one.

Later he sat on the waiting bench in the takeaway. His phone rang and the caller's name came up. Shade. Don't answer, Beth would have said: he's trouble; it always upsets you. He pressed the key and said "When you're wounded and left on Afghanistan's plains …"

"And the women come out to cut up what remains …" responded Shade. "I need you, soldier."

Next day it was raining. Douglas Jones held the front door of the bungalow open on a chain and said "Sorry. I know it's not your fault."

"Send him away!" shrilled a voice inside. "Just send him away!"

Studying the place, paint peeling, newspaper pasted inside the window, garden a mess, the view across marshes to a power-station, Charlie wondered what it had been like when the painter himself had lived there.

Get a man inside, he thought.

"This lad," he indicated Carlos, "needs to use the toilet. We'd be very grateful."

"What?" said the voice inside.

"Toilet," said Douglas.

An indistinguishable reply.

"It's more than a piss," said Charlie.

"More than a piss!" reported Douglas.

"In his trousers!" said the voice.

Douglas bit his lip and nodded.

"But just him," he said. "Two minutes, sorry."

"Thank you," said Charlie. "Very civil of you."

Carlos was admitted and the door closed. Charlie dialled. Tommo, he realised, was using his own mobile to photograph the landscape through the rain-splashed windscreen.

"What's happening?" said Archie Rudolph in Charlie's ear.

Charlie explained.

"Jesus Christ!"

"Give it five," said Charlie.

Behind him the door opened and Douglas yelled "Is that Rudolph? What's he saying? If he says that I signed a—"

Charlie turned, raised a pacifying hand, and although Douglas said "Hey..!" pushed past him into the house, where the newspaper-blocked light was strange and table lamps with cloth shades had different coloured bulbs and Carlos faced a woman across a card table and held her hands in his as she tried not to weep and—

The device went off in the adjacent storehouse and the mud wall flew in and—

"Christ," said Charlie, "What's—"

"What? Charlie? What's—?" said Archie Rudolph.

Charlie's jaw was locked. Breathe, he urged. Fucking breathe.

Something clicked like wax in his ear and he said "Mr Rudolph?"

"What? For God's sake. What? Make a higher offer?"

"Maybe."

"I've already told him we're not liquid, he—"

Silence. Thinking. Everyone stared.

"It's been, like, hospital," said the woman, "and nobody I knew and Douglas was in Africa, weren't you? Was it?"

"I was here," said Douglas.

Carlos spoke Spanish and held her hands to his lips.

"We have a signed contract," said Rudolph. "This can't be serious."

"I know," said Charlie. "But it is."

"It's not an auction, is it? There's not another buyer?"

"I think that's a wise decision for the moment, Mr Rudolph, so I'll hang up and persuade young Douglas to put the kettle on."

He ended the call and turned off the power.

"Mine's black with three sugars," he said. "The lad outside takes milk."

Trev was angry. He threw a plate at the wall. Fragments went everywhere. The kids were scared. He yelled "Shut up!" and dialled 999 to report Cindy missing.

"Mrs Buggy wants to fuck me," said Tommo in the van later, "what should I do?"

Archie Rudolph's client had flown in from St Petersburg, did not speak English, and was accompanied by a thick set man described as a secretary but clearly a bodyguard and a tall, contained and beautiful blonde woman of about thirty who translated and was the art adviser. Once she clicked her fingers when the client picked his nose, and she asked Archie how far they were from a certain shirt maker.

"No distance at all," he said and walked them. The client was delighted. What did I tell you, the interpreter seemed to be saying in Russian.

Archie's mobile rang. He said "Excuse me."

"Sure," said the interpreter.

"It's okay," said Charlie. "All aboard. Happy ever after."

"Where are you?"

"Pitstop."

Some greasy-spoon van in a layby, surmised Archie. Why are the working-class like that? And then: there is no traditional working-class anymore; just millions of confused people.

"Can you stay open late?" said Charlie.

Back at the van Tommo said "You haven't advised me."

"How can we, if we don't know Mrs Buggy?"

Carlos grinned and repeated proverbs in Spanish.

Archie disliked large format mobile phones because whatever pocket one put them in they distorted the line of a suit; but at least they gave a good-sized image of a painting.

"Tell me what you think of this," he said.

He leaned to the interpreter, and she to him. A wisp of her hair caressed him for a moment. He was aware of her scent.

Looking at the screen she said "My God. Is this what I think? When was it painted?"

"Nineteen fifty," said Archie.

"How big is it?"

"He couldn't afford canvas so he took a door off its hinges and painted her on that. Then they left without paying the rent."

"They were lovers."

"They were."

"But I recognise. She is the one who was as well painted by—"

"Yes."

She looked at him. Her eyes had violet in them. Archie thought: be careful.

"So she is the girl in the scandal."

"Yes."

"She go to prison."

"Yes."

"But it should have been him? So she keep his pictures?"

"The ones he abandoned. Yes."

There was an interruption in Russian about cufflinks; but from the glance the client gave him Archie knew that she had explained, and the bait been taken.

"We could," said Charlie, "but I don't fancy it." Meaning – take the blanket-wrapped door down the twisty gallery stairs. They were tired after the day and their concentration might slip, whereas Archie was bouncy: the salesman's thrill at his own improvisations.

He had already phoned his wife and said "Buzz! Buzz!"

Sometimes they played old vinyl and did the Twist naked: you had a champagne glass in one hand and if you spilled any paid a forfeit.

That they were both over sixty they did not care.

The van was too tall to fit in the garage at the back of the flats so Charlie always parked end-on outside. He sat for a moment. South Armagh. He had put his foot down and China fired at the gun-flashes. Charlie ached. A shower. Beth in the shower shouting "Hit me! Hit me!" She never entered his flat again and he never wanted her to. What they had both wanted was the meetings without obligations or even spending an entire night together: the pure sex. But now what? He took a breath and texted her.

In Rome it was four in the morning. Vittorio removed his shoes at the door of the flat and crept in. All in darkness. Thank God. Then a light clicked on and Cesare was waiting and accusatory.

He noted Vittorio's cut lip and said "This cannot proceed."

"Your arse," hissed Vittorio. "Your miserable penis that smells like an ashtray."

"You are fifty years old. You destroy your mother's happiness."

"…!"

A wet fart noise.

Not actual lovers for seventeen years, but still a household: Vittorio, his mother, and Cesare, who did the cooking.

Vittorio bowed. Cesare returned it and turned off the light. They went to their separate rests, in Cesare's case a camp bed erected each night in the living room.

In London's early hours did Mrs Buggy return from night duty, sit at the end of Tommo's bed and repeat in a whisper a conversation between herself, a dying patient and Mary the Mother of God? Hold on there, your boat's casting off now, can't you feel it rock, and is he Yours yet, Mother, is he Yours? Now, she was asleep and had left her door open. The house creaked even when it was silent, and Tommo pissed into the side of the bowl so that there would be no loud splashing.

Notting Hill. Expensive terraces. Beth's shop a block away. She suggested the gastropub but when she walked in knew that its lunchtime clatter was wrong. People at laptops. Mothers with child buggies. Spritzers. Charlie in work gear looked awkward. She made bright chatter.

"My God. Is she still beautiful? Did you take a photo?"

"No."

"Why not?"

"Her dementia."

"She's scared?"

"Very."

A waiter brought bruschettas and said "Hi, Beth. Any decisions yet?"

"Pending," she said.

"Black pepper?"

"Thanks."

"I'll be back."

Decisions?

"How did Archie know about her?"

"She was on a TV doco years ago."

"He remembered?"

Across the street, Charlie saw, were a builder's rubbish chute, skip and portaloo.

"How did Archie *become* Rudolph and Rudiger?"

"What?"

"Well. Who *is* Rudiger?"

"Doesn't he run the gallery in Cologne?"

"Was he the money?"

What did she mean: decisions? Charlie managed to ask.

"Didn't I tell you?"

"What?"

Her phone pinged.

"I said—"

The waiter. Lean back. Rasp. Black pepper. Enjoy.

"Thank you, darling ..."

"Shangri-la ..." replied the waiter over his shoulder.

Children misbehaved. Women talked.

Beth put the phone in her handbag.

Charlie stared at her.

"The shop," she said. "Young refurbers. I think I need to update."

None of these people around us know anything about history, she said, so they don't want to pretend they live in it. More minimalism, darling, with a few vulgar blocks of colour.

Charlie described other dealers' shops, but she already knew.

"And anyway, I could make the actual shop a downstairs sitting-room, and put everything online."

She hadn't meant to say that, and pretended not to hear his question. They were silent.

Later, in the street, she having refused an amaretto, he thought to ask: "Where will you buy new stock?"

"There's a man in Rome. He drives round on a scooter."

"Rome?"

She showed him the phone: a photo of a coffee table.

"Christ!" said Charlie, because a parking attendant was staring at the van.

Beth's friend Wendy had been minding the shop and achieved a small sale. She was a billowy woman whose children were at boarding school, and she did not ask about lunch but waited until Beth said "Disaster. My fault."

"How?"

"Choked. Both of us."

In Rome, crash-helmeted, Vittorio clicked again on a Murano vase.

"But what that means, darling," said Wendy, "is that he's as desperate as you are."

Ping. The vase.

"My God. It's a Carlo Scarpa. I mean, can I afford it, and would I ever find a proper buyer?"

"He's not just pinging you, though, is he darling?" said Wendy. "He's pinging New York and everywhere."

Cindy was in a doorway in Watford. She had a cut head and was drunk. The ambulance man said what's your name? Mary Jane. Where d'you live? Down the grid. What's your number? Cucumber. What's your station? She couldn't remember but he did. Eggs and bacon.

Tommo was excited. He enlarged the photos he'd taken through the rain-blotched windscreen and daubed over them fantasy nudes of Mrs Buggy. Britain's past, and the way it was now, and how he felt blank about it. No connections. Which was a sort of connection, he realised, between his talent for representation and the ideas-art towards which his tutors pushed him.

"I suppose it's sex," said Mrs Macauley. "It always is, isn't it, whatever else they say? Sex or money."

"Yes," said Charlie.

"Knowing you," she smiled. "I can't believe it's money."

"No."

Each failed to looked at the other.

He had driven up overnight and not warned her. She wore an old-fashioned housecoat to dust. When Charlie was young the bungalow had overlooked fields but now there were houses.

"So can you tell me, then, or what?" she said.

He heard a voice not his own say "Violence ..."

"We meet for sex, really. We don't share much else. It's how she ... And I'm ... D'you know what I mean?"

She began to reply but did not.

Then she said "But now she wants ...?" and gestured, as though at all the worn possessions around her.

To her he could say what he suspected.

"What do *you* want?"

He didn't know.

"Well, to get it off your chest, at least."

"Yes."

"You've not come up just for this, have you?"

"Suddenly decided. Middle of the night."

Boys, she thought. Impatience. I don't know.

"Well," she said, "you'd best have a lie down in your old room, hadn't you?"

His old room. Decades after he used it. Look how old he is, and seen all those dreadful things, and only just starting to grow up.

Later she made baked beans on toast and topped them with poached eggs and said "Do you want to stop over?"

"Better not," he said. "I've missed two jobs as it is."

She gossiped about people he'd known and how Bangladeshi women in the town weren't allowed to go out to work, and many of them still couldn't speak English.

"And you wouldn't recognise it," she said. "Everything pulled down and different."

"I know," he said. "I don't."

At which he knew that he wanted to stay over, and did, and before they went to bed she made cocoa the way she used to, and they talked about Mr Macauley and she said "You don't regret it all, do you?"

"The army?"

"Yes."

"No."

"Serving your country."

"Whatever that is now."

Out of the silence he said "I'll try to come up more often."

"I am lucky, though," she said. "All the friends I've made through the choir."

*

103

Then having talked to her Charlie knew what he must do and what he wanted and the excitement of it kept him awake so that at dawn he phoned. Beth answered and they told each other the truth. "I'll come now," he said, but she said "No point. I'll tell you when." He lay in bushes before an advance across open ground but for the first time it seemed far away. He knew that he had strength and in the morning drove to Manchester, to pick up Shade and drive him to London. On the motorway texts pinged. Sorry. Had to give the job to someone else. Where are you? No use to me. Sorry.

"You're sprauncy, though," said Shade. "Good times with Beth?"

"She had to go off somewhere, actually."

"Any place we know?"

Charlie told him. Shade swigged from a bottle of gin.

"Funny thing," he said. "Could never drink it neat before. Just shows."

More pings and a confirmed job. It would need two of the lads. Maybe three. Charlie tried Ahmed again but there was no message. Just a long buzz and a cut off. So he called Tiff.

Rich people's vanity, thought Charlie. Jesus Christ. In Holland Park a party marquee would be erected over an entire garden. Canvas over the trees and water feature and a dance floor over the grass. Among the branches and on special easels would sit paintings, which it was Charlie's job to collect.

"Beyond!" muttered Tiff. "They call these paintings?"

Some were pastiches of abstraction, but others were famous images photocopied on canvas, and they were one of the fashion-shoot, rock-show and catwalk designer Leonard's stocks-in-trade.

"He can do a funeral as well," said Charlie, nodding at baroque Madonnas, and Leonard himself, tall, white-haired, the sleeves of his shirt and cashmere rolled above his elbows, ended his phone call and said "Charlie! Splendissimo! Sorry about that. My partner. You remember him. He's in a play at Watford and can't understand why nobody's reviewed it."

"Why haven't they?" said Charlie.

A gesture: why are these things so obvious and why does nobody recognise them?

"We're thick," said Charlie. "You'll have to tell us."

"Falling sales, dear. Loss of revenue to digital. Papers can only review what's paid for. It's why there's page upon page of women's fashion and no book reviews. Now – what we didn't add over the phone was that on top of the pictures and the lanterns—"

Tiff was quizzical, he realised, and stopped.

"Sorry," she said, "but what is paid for?"

He brought it back into his mind.

"Theatre wise? The West End. Buy ads and you get reviewed. Not that they actually need reviews anymore. It's all word of Facebook, Twitter and what-not. Ludicrous. Same with art galleries of course. Who reviews them the way they did when we were young?"

This time it was Tiff's grin.

"Well," he said, "when I was young. And what I was about to say is that I bought in a mound of carnival masks and cloaks and we'll need those to go as well. We out-contract the flowers."

"When I leave school," said Cindy, "I want to be a long-distance lorry driver. But it may not happen."

"Why not?"

"I'm too popular. Other girls can be jealous, you know."

"Right," said the doctor. "And can you still not remember what your name is?"

*

105

They were finished at the party house by mid-afternoon and returned next morning to collect. Catering staff were still packing up and one said "Careful. We've had drama."

"Drama?"

The packer rolled his eyes. Last night's hostess had arrived and glared at everyone. She wore emerald pants, a shirt with cleavage, and six inch heels.

"In the morning?" said Tiff. "At her age?"

"Shut up," said Charlie.

They eased a laser-printed Monet to a bed of bubble.

"She's wired," continued Tiff.

Zip went Carlos with gaffer tape.

"The husband's in the House of Lords," said Charlie.

"That's it," said Tiff. "That's your actual drugs problem."

"Just get here!" said the hostess into her mobile, and to no-one in particular, "What's wrong with people? Why is every single thing a problem?"

Later, as they boarded the van, a black youth propped his push-bike against the railings. He was hooded.

"There you go," said Tiff. "The delivery."

There was another bling job next day, but it began badly, with a parking jam at the back of the auction house: two pantechnicons, one of the drivers very agitated, an expostulating Traffic Warden, and a dirt-stained working Land Rover, its owner a man in tweeds holding an old equestrian painting, and trying not to shout at the Warden.

"Santa Maria!" said Carlos.

Charlie double-parked.

"I'll get out and suss it," said Tiff, and scrambled over Carlos. She was black and graceful and wore a belted overall jumpsuit.

"She look like test pilot," said Carlos. "If only she fly me."

"She's about to be married," said Charlie, "to her girlfriend who's a much older woman."

Tiff did an unexpected high five with one of the pantechnicon men and strolled to overhear the argument between the Warden and the man in tweeds. She held up a hand to stop them, and asked a question.

The man replied. A blocked car hooted.

The Warden tried not to seem powerless.

Tiff touched the man, lightly, for sympathy, and returned. Carlos wound down his window.

"His wife's missing," said Tiff. "Run off with a jockey."

"Why's he come here with his picture?"

"Displacement activity."

"What about the vans?"

"Two men inside the building but their phones aren't working."

"You two go in for the item," said Charlie. "If we're moved on I'll wait around that corner."

The item was a 1730 gold-framed Venetian mirror and the buyer Mary lived in Chelsea Harbour. She said "Thanks a million, Charlikins, I may need you again very soon." She had sparkle dust on one cheekbone, a view of the river, and purple velvet curtains.

"Beyond comment," said Tiff as they drove away. "Crash-hot beyond."

Cindy asked to see the doctor again. She had forgotten to tell him about her hamster, who was in her classroom desk and would need to be fed.

"After this," said Fat Percy, "how would you fancy a holiday in Penzance?"

"This" had been a trip to Hackney, and an empty factory awaiting planning permission for demolition and the erection of a block of smart flats. Young artists squatted there for studio space. Percy had spotted one of them at her Art College Degree Show and sent Charlie for two of her pieces on approval. No promises. Just stick one in the gallery and see if anyone noticed.

"Penzance?"

"The auction house."

"Off-loading?"

"Allowing good work to breathe again," said Adrian.

"With a stopover in Wincanton."

"For the jump races?"

"For Mary Sheridan Fine Art Limited."

More off-loading of small stuff that wouldn't sell, knew Charlie.

"It's at least one overnight," surmised Adrian.

"As I say, a holiday," beamed Percy, and Charlie said "Let me check the diary."

"Diary?"

"Phone," said Adrian. "Everything's digitalised."

"God forbid," said Percy

"I can fit it in," conceded Charlie, thinking: alone: not knowing: on the road's better than the flat.

In Wincanton bustling Mary Sheridan said "How's Beth? Had botox yet?" and before he could answer "Joking. How is she really?" and he said "Blooming," but with a hollowness, and he thought she detected it.

Then in Penzance he bought a takeaway and slept in the van and rain drummed on the roof. He remembered bivouacs and having to lie next to dead bodies and texted Beth IN VAN RAIN ON ROOF but knew that on that evening in particular she would not reply. He thought about Mrs Macauley. Where was it they went every year? Prestatyn? But she'd like Penzance. I should have brought her. These sudden quiet streets at the top of the town. Their oddness. She'd have put her finger on it.

As he left the auction house next morning he saw an argument in the street. A woman tried to stop a teenager running away from her. She shouted at people. "It's social media! They won't bloody let her alone!" But the girl wrestled a push-bike from its startled owner and pedalled off. The woman ran after. The bike owner said could someone make a phone call for him.

On Bodmin Moor Charlie stopped in a lay-by. Vehicles whizzed past him. Clouds soared. He wanted to phone but knew that he mustn't and took deep breaths. The air tingled. He felt clean even though he'd not had a shower, and used café lavatories. Then he thought: tomorrow: think about this bloody awful job on Friday.

Ernest Hannaway himself had suggested the time, and Charlie knew why: it was when Hannaway hoped that his wife would be out shopping. Iffy, thought Charlie, and he was right. It went wrong.

The paintings were smallish and in storage in Brentford. Charlie loaded them alone because there was a signal failure on the Northern Line and Tommo and Tiff were delayed at opposite ends. "I'll meet you on the way," he said, but they were late and there was no time to brief them properly. So Mrs Hannaway arrived when they were unloading and her anger filled the mews.

She ran, long white hair, sneakers, jeans, a haversack, and screamed at Tiff.

"Stop it, you black bitch!"

"There's no call for that, Viv," said Ernest.

But Viv swung the haversack. Tiff blocked it with a stiff arm.

"Classic Ninja!" said Tommo.

Viv's shopping spilled out.

"Sorry, Mrs Hannaway. Your eggs are broken."

Charlie was decisive. An arm round a shoulder. A polite but cautionary voice. They heard the wails and his sympathy as they unloaded the last of 16 paintings. Carrying one in Tiff said "How was Penzance, by the way? I forgot to ask?"

"The seagulls all asked after you, and while you're at it bring in Mrs Hannaway's shopping."

Then because they had all hated the job Charlie took them for a pizza.

"Sorry I joked," said Tiff. "I felt rotten."

Tommo said "He was *the* Ernest Hannaway, right?"

"He is."

The last alive of the English painters who responded in an important way to Abstract Expressionism. Venice Biennale at age twenty-three. Big sales and high life. Then he lost it. Stopped painting. Disappeared.

"Disappeared?"

"Well, he didn't literally disappear," said Charlie. "He worked in a bar in Alicante. Then he had health issues. Came back. Found he could paint again. So the gallery kick-started things."

"Kick-started?"

"Put stuff into auction. Bought it themselves at fake prices. All that."

"So why did they get rid of him?"

"He kept breaking his contract."

"Contract?"

"They didn't mind him selling on the side. They just asked for steady prices and some commission."

"Commission ..." said Tommo.

"There was stuff on eBay and his wife lost the plot with everybody and so ..."

And so they had an artmover return the paintings.

Tiff began to speak but stopped and they were silent. That woman's life, thought Tiff. What she imagined would be glamour and respect for integrity. Drunk tourists in Spain. Her menopause. No children. And I need advice, realised Tommo, but they don't teach the business side at College. Charlie pulled himself together and went to pay, and Hannaway himself, thought Tiff, old and not there at all, somehow, except for the cataract-blurred blue of his eyes. She wanted to return and ask him things, but knew she never could.

Tommo recovered his jacket from the dry-cleaners but was mistaken: the now blurred lottery ticket was not a winning line so he glued it to MRS BUGGY NUMBER 7, which was a collage over a blow-up of her ankles, taken on his phone as she emptied the spin-dryer.

Charlie ached to phone. He ached to know. But she'd said "You do it your way. Let me do it mine." Which was her dignity, and the test she'd set for him. And for four days there were no jobs, not even the shit ones that came more often these days. Then there was a call. Australian Greg. "The time's come," he said. "I need you to give me an estimate."

"In the days of the empire," said Australian Greg, "we'd go to Paris, come back with a car-load and sell it very quickly for twice what it cost us."

"Three times," said Charlie.

"Not always."

Charlie's phone went. Adrian at Fat Percy's.

"Charlie? Rush job. Crisis. This afternoon. Percy says can you do it?"

"Er …"

"Where are you?"

"Pimlico Road."

"Not *the* Pimlico Road? Where antique dealers go when they die?"

At the gallery Percy said "You mean it's just you? No other muscle?"

"I wasn't moving Greg. I was discussing the logistics."

"Greg?"

"Twentieth Century Decorative."

"Him?"

"And what he's decided to stop selling."

"Enough said," adjudged Percy

"Enough. What's the gig?"

It was to take a cheque to another dealer and bring back a sculpture.

"Are you insured up to this value?" said the dealer.

"No."

"Why does Percy keep risking it?"

"He's lonely," said the dealer's wife. "Divorce again. Rattling about in a big house."

"Or maybe he's like you Charlie, eh?" said the dealer. "Sentimental about the world as it used to be."

Later his wife said he shouldn't have said that. The specialist packers and internet delivery firms wouldn't touch raw nerve jobs and that's why the likes of Charlie got them. To make up for what they'd lost. And for all we know Percy eats at Scott's every night, and not just when he takes us for an oyster. Not that we should worry, having the artists to do Palm Beach and Basel when he hasn't.

There was room in the cab so Trev thought sod school and took the kids with him. Blanket each. Packets of crisps. Two plastic bottles to piss in. When he delivered the lorry he had them hide round the corner. Home on the train and then they did it again. They had stuff on their phones, anyway. What other solution was there? Even his own sister in Hastings had said that it wasn't convenient to take them.

They had waited in their car at the garages and got out as Charlie parked the van. He knew at once what they were.

"How long have you been there?" he said.

"We won't keep you a minute, Mr March."

They had a photo of Ahmed.

"I know," said Charlie. "I phoned him. But he never replied. Were you listening?"

"When did you last see him?"

"What's he done?"

"Disappeared."

"Did he ever, at any time," said the thin one, "give you any indication that—"

Charlie tried not to show what he realised: that Ahmed wasn't their quarry. He was their informant, and they'd lost him.

"—he had concerns about his safety?"

"Well. He lived in the squat with about nineteen come-and-go people, didn't he?"

"He worried about them?"

"His belongings. There were more than he could fit in one backpack."

They stared. They trusted him, but not beyond a certain point. But they gave him a phone number. Then the thin one looked back and said "Why did you work with him, actually?"

Enough, he thought, and said "Wasn't it your lot who put him on to me?"

Silence.

"And I could see that he needed the money ..."

They understood, and so did he. Ahmed had felt unsafe, not trusted them, and done another runner. Then his phone pinged. They indicated. Check it.

"An armoire," he said. "Repaired. Ready to be collected."

"What's an armoire?"

"Don't be stupid," said the one at the car. "It's a fucking armoire, isn't it?"

When Charlie delivered it Wendy was alone in the shop.

"Called away, dear. Exeter. Her cousin's had a fall."

She doesn't know we've spoken, realised Charlie. And if that's the cover story it's a bad one. Beth doesn't have a cousin in Exeter. In Scarborough, but not in Exeter. He said nothing, though, as Wendy looked at him and thought: he's too stretched: would he kill himself without the pills from Beth's private doctor?

Then it was September and Tommo, Carlos and Tiff went back to college.

"Which fucks you for the Art Fair," said China.

"Which is why I've dropped round," confessed Charlie.

114

Because China knew the removals casuals who might be up for the get-ins and get-outs. He suggested some.

"Perfect. Plus I've already got young Harry."

"Harry?"

"Wannabe big-deal estate agent. On his uppers. Phoned and asked for a favour."

"Why's he on his uppers?"

"He was sacked for fucking."

"Wow!" said Mrs China. "Tell all!"

"What in today's world does one have to do," complained Fat Percy, "to get anything done to any sort of standard at all?"

He had ordered the larger wing of the stand to be painted one colour and the smaller another, to display his chosen stock to best effect; but the contractors had done it the wrong way round.

"I mean, these mounts against that background could induce vomit," said Percy, and Charlie said "I can take away now and bring new stuff later."

"We don't have a slot."

Meaning that the Fair organisers rationed each exhibitor's unloading time, parking was a nightmare, and there was often what China called furniture gridlock.

"But I'm coming back," said Charlie, "for New Avenues."

"New Avenues?"

"Shoreditch. Very smart young man."

Percy seemed about to speak but didn't.

"On the other hand," put in Harry, "you could just hang the pictures meant for that wall over there. And vice versa."

Adrian folded his arms in a smug sort of way

Percy said "Are you the one who was sacked for fucking?"

"As a matter of fact," said Harry, "I think it might look good on my CV."

*

In the van Charlie said "What I never did ask was the girl's age."

Harry stared ahead. A cyclist gave them the finger even though they were stuck at the lights.

"London's very charming, isn't it?" said Harry.

"The girl."

"Gym mistress. First job. She's very bendy."

Early evening slots meant that the exhibitors setting-up stayed late, but at least the vans could linger. When they had delivered for New Avenues Charlie's casuals sloped off but Harry said "Wander round?" Charlie, thinking "Christ, he is like Jack Shade," said "Why not?"

Percy was there, and had re-organised.

"It's better than your original idea," said Harry. "There's more space around the Nicholson."

"We're having a glass of Chablis," said Percy. "Why don't I throw yours in your face?"

He looked tired, and Charlie felt it. Noises that should have echoed didn't, absorbed by the partitions and the gauze of the false ceiling. Percy topped up the drinks and they gossiped. A Sandra Blow balanced the Nicholson, and as they stared at it Harry wandered off, glass in hand.

Some stands were dressed, and a few still setting-up. Electricians were up ladders. Harry said "Hello" to a sniffer dog but the handler snapped "Don't touch him!". Behind Harry a voice he knew said "Trust you!"

"Stinker?"

"Is it true that old Willoughby sacked you?"

They had opened the innings together in minor public-school House Matches, and got pissed at numerous reunions.

"Is that your father on the stand? How is he?"

One of two expensively suited men in front of a Grand Tour portrait.

"Is the other bloke a client?"

"Not exactly," said Stinker, and explained.

"Crikey…"

Later, Harry told Charlie about the man, and why he was there.

"Your mate shouldn't have told you that, should he? Not really."

"Well. His nickname is Stinker."

But it's not exactly that he's a Stinker, thought Charlie. It's more a conviction that because they're superior it doesn't matter. Like an officer he'd known, who could only be killed by silver bullets. Then a bomb full of ball-bearings shredded him.

Which did not stop Charlie telling Percy, who was wry and said "Eyes peeled, then, for the announcement…"

The end of the Art Fair entailed deliveries, one of which was an Ivan Hitchens up a spiral staircase: one man held the left side and right bottom corner of the frame, another on the staircase held the top right, and Charlie instructed. Half a pace. Steady. Swivel. Go up a rung. Swivel. Repeat. It was a Knightsbridge mews and the owners had dug out the basement and added a floor. They tipped Charlie a hundred in cash.

When the police stopped Trev he was driving a transporter with six Smart Cars on it to a dealership in Berwick-on-Tweed. The kids, their faces war-painted with Cindy's left-behind make-up, were in a car on the lower deck of the transporter. It was their spacecraft, they said, and inside they were weightless.

"Weightless …" said the Social Worker who took them to the hostel, and thought: does this mean that he gave them drugs?

It was a drive down the A3 to Portsmouth, and a super-yacht moored at Gunwharf Quays.

"You'll need one other person at this end," said Willie Wishart, "but at the other they'll do the lifting themselves."

Charlie began to speak but a phone rang. Wishart patted his pinstripes to locate it.

"Percy? What - ? No. No, I haven't – Oh. Oh dear …"

He stopped the call and turned to the young woman at the desk.

"Hermione, you couldn't pop out with some petty cash and buy the *Telegraph*, could you?" And to Charlie: "Mary Wallace died. There's an obit."

"It'll be online," said Hermione. "I can print it out."

"But if we had the actual rag I'd have the crossword, wouldn't I?"

He must be eighty, thought Charlie, and it must be true: they have sold the gallery to a hedge fund, and Willie's just here as a front. Or because he can't think of what else to do. And he's shrunk. His collar's half a size too big.

"Mary Wallace?"

"I'll print it out anyway, Mr Wishart. There's *The Times* as well."

"I hate them all," said Willie. "What did you say?"

"Mary Wallace," repeated Charlie.

"Oh. Yes. Legends. She ran the Arts Council's touring shows. Stuff went all over the place. Wherever you lived you could follow what was going on. And we could make suggestions: help along a newcomer's reputation. I think I'll sit down."

The gallery lobby had leather and steel benches, like a boutique hotel.

"And the papers reviewed everything," continued Willie, "but today they don't. So it's a mess and we're blamed and called elitist …"

Hermione handed him the print-outs.

"Does it say about her affair with whatshisface? I bet it doesn't."

They watched him as he scanned the obituaries.

" 'A woman who saw her mission as art for all ..." he quoted. "Very good."

He looked at Charlie over the top of his spectacles.

"I was in the Royal Academy's ghetto-blaster last week and ..."

"Blockbuster," muttered Hermione.

"Blockbuster," he acknowledged, "and people didn't so much look at pictures as photograph themselves with a painting in the background. Art for all indeed. So the sad fact is that I don't care about them anymore, not even when ..."

"When what?" said Charlie.

"When a de Kooning gets taken to a money launderer's super-yacht in Portsmouth, and disappears for ever ..."

"Oh, come on! Come on! Same old argument. Thatcher this and Thatcher that, and she's the reason London's a mess and Britain's broken. Bollocks!" said the florid man holding a gin and tonic.

"I suppose you voted for her," said the grand-daughter, who had been introduced as Molly.

"What's that got to do with it?"

"What I've said for thirty years, to which you've never listened, is that ..." attempted grandmother Eileen.

"Gordon Brown. Do-gooder. Tony Blair. Thank you very much for the Iraq War."

It was an evening hanging job given them by Gary the dealer. Two old clients who had retired to the Algarve. But husband John had a medical condition so they came home.

"I did warn them about Battersea," said Gin and Tonic to the ceiling, "but no, no, so here they are in a shoe box."

"Unlike you I have our mother's very neat feet," said Eileen.

"Ha ha."

"How can it be so awful," said Molly, "when millions of people go to Tate Modern?"

"Curator art," said Gin and Tonic. "Video installations about trans-gender lavatories."

He was an actor, realised Charlie, and remembered seeing him on the telly.

"Are all families like this?" said Molly, and to Tommo "Super tee-shirt, by the way."

But would a girl like this get off with me, thought Tommo.

"Drill," said Charlie, looking at his little pencilled cross on the wall.

Tommo handed it and thought drill, drill, I think I could drill golly Miss Molly.

"Are you all right?" said Eileen to husband John.

"I think I'll sit down, if that's okay."

"I'll pour you another," said Gin and Tonic.

Eileen looked daggers.

"The doctor said it's okay," said John. "He said what's the difference, didn't he?"

Shoe-box, thought Charlie. He's right. Too many pictures for the space.

He raised the point of the drill to the cross, and switched on.

Next day he saw Greg, who said "How was it?"

"It was fine."

"Were they at each other's throats?"

"Er ..."

"Was Richard drunk?"

He must mean the actor.

"I wouldn't say drunk, exactly, no."

"What would you say?"

"I'm the picture hanger. I wouldn't say anything."

"Oh, go on."

"Topped up..?" compromised Charlie.

Greg nodded.

"Shouldn't smile, though, really. When the mother died he couldn't cope, so John said 'You'd better come to me and your sister.'"

"He's been with them ever since?"

"Arguing all day every day," said Greg. "When can you start?"

His shop lease ended with the month and he had already exchanged contracts on his flat. His new boyfriend was twenty-six years younger and wouldn't leave Brisbane.

"I'm fed up with fucking Lalique anyway," he said.

"Plus what's in the basement," said Charlie.

"The basement."

A half day loading. Drive to the auction house in Salisbury. Unload. Back by midnight. He'd need one other person.

Tommo had been told by her grandmother that Miss Molly worked in a design shop in Barnes and he stood across the street and watched her through the window. Then she came out to buy lunchtime sandwiches. He ran and caught her eye but it was blank and she walked on without a sign of recognition. He started to follow but a passer-by was staring. Tommo said "Oh fuck!" and hailed a taxi that he could not afford.

Greg was surprised by the man Charlie brought to help clear the shop: far too posh, dearie, he thought. There must be a story. He gave them pink champagne in paper cups.

Cindy's case was discussed for an hour at the Psychiatric Team meeting, and opinion was divided, between those who thought that she was hiding her identity, and those who thought that she was traumatised and had inadvertently suppressed it.

*

As he and Harry drove back from Salisbury Charlie was texted about a new job and thought it perfect for Tiff, and that because it was an evening call she'd be free. When he phoned her she said "What d'you mean – it's back to the bling?"

"Chelsea Harbour," he said. "Wardrobe detox."

"The furniture, or the clothes?"

They arrived at about seven and the stylist, wine glass in hand, opened the door and said "Thank God. I can't get the next bottle open."

"Where's Mary?"

A wavy gesture. They followed it. Mary, glitter on the other cheek this time, was snoring on top of a mound of clothes.

In the sitting-room Charlie said "When did you start on the booze?"

"Mary? Before I got here."

"Crikey."

"Well. A detox is a crisis, isn't it?" she said.

"I dunno. Is it?"

"Your clothes are your ..." she burped. "Sorry ... identity, but some person comes and tells you to throw them all out."

"We have to carry her very gently into the other bedroom and ..."

"I mean, everything she owned was inapp – inapp ..."

"Inappropriate," said Tiff.

"... and most of it wasn't even ..."

"Why don't you get some fresh air on the balcony?" said Charlie.

"Whereas in fact, I said to her, you may be too puffy but basically you've got a dignified life ... What?"

Charlie indicated.

"Balcony. Thank you."

She was tight-lipped. She stood up but sagged down again and said "I always ask for the money up front."

"Seen the mirror?" said Tiff.

"I know," said Charlie.

The Venetian mirror they had delivered had been painted a garish sky-blue.

"Curtains …" said the Stylist.

"She thought it matched them?" said Tiff.

Another belch and a nod.

"It doesn't," said Tiff.

"Come on," said Charlie, and they carried Mary as carefully as they could. She half woke and said "Charliekins! Kissikins … Oh my God!" and Tiff said "I think she's pissed herself."

"On the clothes?"

"Not sure."

Later, they were slumped in the van and Tiff said "What's the back story?"

"She was a client of Beth's."

Tiff waited.

"Girl from the suburbs. You know. Good looker. Bright. She married an Arab."

"An Arab?"

"A very heavy-duty Saudi. She lived there. She had a courtyard with tame gazelles and unbelievable money and… Lots of them drink, of course, but with her it was ludicrous …"

"He dumped her."

"In a very civilised way."

"Kids?"

"Grown up. Ashamed of her."

Tiff snorted.

"Beth used to go out with her."

"Go out?"

"Dinners."

"Right."

"And the other Saudi ex-wives. The husbands have accounts at big hotels."

Big hotels, thought Tiff. Have I ever been in a big hotel?

"But the dinners had a price cap. The exes could only spend so much, so … you know."

"No."

"Mary had arguments with all the head waiters. Made scenes. Etcetera …"

Tiff's lover, or older wife, as she liked to call herself, was thin with wild grey hair and long frocks that would have been cutting-edge at Woodstock, and a regretful sort of humour about people who didn't agree with her.

"Where've you been?" she said. "It's my night at the food bank."

"I know. Wait. Let me tell you," said Tiff.

"Kiss me. Then I can think about you while I help all those unlucky people …"

Tiff was rough with her, and felt the nipples harden.

"You've got to wear a bra, Mrs Elaine Madison," she said, "before they crash to the floor."

"You'll be down there with them, though, won't you?" said Elaine, who had retained the house in Hornsey when she booted her husband out. Not that she had ever dreamed that it would be worth about a million. She taught English History at a comprehensive where almost none of the pupils cared about English History, seeing themselves, if they looked at it at all, as its victims; which Elaine encouraged. She was alone but happy, and involved in causes and committees. Then one day Tiff arrived in her A stream.

They were at once secret and intoxicated lovers. Then I saw her mind go zoom, Elaine marvelled. Wow!

From school Tiff went to Fashion College and moved in. Her older brother was in a gang and called her a batty bitch. But he was wary of her quick mind and she always thought: is he like the father I don't know because he left us?

"No, no," said her mother, "is you that is like him."

Whatever that meant. Litter and graffiti. Filthy roller doors.

Dead condoms. Where does reading books get you anyway, that's what I'd like to know. It's getting me out, thought Tiff, and then I can get Mum out and—

Next day, as Charlie lugged the clothes into a Charity shop, she phoned him.

"Sorry, Forgot to tell you last night."

"What?"

"Toothpaste and brush"

"What?"

"Found them in the van."

Charlie hesitated.

"They must have got mixed up with the clothes. Bin them."

"Okay. See you."

But she'd found them before the clothes went in, and they were held in an elastic band. Someone, she realised, had been sleeping in the van.

"Seen the trade papers?" said Percy.

"No."

"It probably made the posh nationals, actually."

"I don't read the posh nationals," said Charlie.

"Never?"

"Sports sections sometimes ..."

"There you are again, you see, creeping philistinism."

"What are you actually talking about?" said Charlie.

"Your fornicating friend Harry," put in Adrian.

"Harry?" Then he realised. "Oh..!"

*

The job for Percy was a Saturday morning delivery to a young couple who had moved into a flat overlooking railway lines at Woking Station. The wife was blonde and pretty and wearing a track suit and said "Wow! Oh, wow! Roddy – it's the picture!" and to Charlie "Never bought one before. Can't afford this, really. It's on the drip."

Roddy came from the shower with a towel round him. He had curly black hair and grinned and said "Hi" and his wife said "Can you stay and look at it?"

"Sure," said Charlie. He helped them unwrap. What furniture they had was new and the rooms were full of light. They propped the painting against the sofa and stared at it.

It was beautiful and they were very happy and held hands and Charlie envied them. In the van he almost cried and thought Christ. Christ I need love. I need – He needed Beth, but he couldn't go to her yet. Not until she called him to her.

"I'll buy you a sandwich ..." said Percy, which he did, in a pub in a passage that had fast-food shops, dry cleaners, the back door of a bespoke shoe and boot maker and a gallery selling ancient art. "... and then we can have a gander."

The gander was at Stinker's father's painting, newly identified and authenticated as the work of a sixteenth century Master. It had been bought in an obscure auction for four figures and was now worth several million. It depicted Christ and Saint Veronica and was gently spot-lit on an easel in front of velvet curtains. Admission to the gallery was free as usual, but as well as leaflets about the painting there was a collection box for the Venice in Peril fund.

Percy put a tenner in the box, congratulated the girl behind the desk and a cocky young man he assumed to be Stinker, but did not address as such, and in the street again said "Nice work if you can get it, I suppose ..."

For the authenticating expert, he meant, who had been flown in, put up at Claridge's, wined, dined, provided with a sophisticated female escort (which is what Stinker should not have revealed) and would receive a percentage when the painting was auctioned in New York. "Or," said Percy, "sold to some deluded bugger in the Gulf…"

Mrs Buggy said "What's the matter with you? Look at you. You're not yourself. Is it love?"

Tommo, surprised, said "No."

"Are you sure?"

"Yes."

"Then why are you spreading jam on your sketchbook?"

I have to find him. I have to know where Shade's gone. How would he do it? We're on patrol. Maybe decoyed. What would he do? Relive it. Think it again. So Charlie left the flat, got in the van, and wrapped himself in the blankets used to protect. They smelled of polish and restorer's wax and of Shade himself. Dribbles of curry sauce and piss and liquor and did he spew out toothpaste slime as well? No. He had bottled water, and rinsed. He pissed into other bottles and emptied them down the drain and he shat – I think he shat into newspaper, scrunched it, and shoved it on the skip where they were ripping out the old pub and making flats. Charlie swallowed a retch and deep-breathed. For a moment he had been Shade, in control but not, interested in the loss of it as though it were map-reading, with secrets still, and back-up secrets and where the hell is he?

*

Cindy woke up in a strange room and thought 'Where am I? Where are the kids? Is Trev getting their breakfast? What—?'

Tommo lay on the pavement outside the shop and passers-by ignored him. He could have been dying of an overdose for all they cared. They hurried with their rucksacks and phones and women driving four-by-fours argued over parking spots. Then Miss Molly came out of the shop and kicked him.

"What are you doing? You want to upskirt me, don't you? What are you doing?"

He tried to sit up but she hit his shoulder and off-balanced him.

"Stop it! Ow! Stop it!"

"How dare you? In front of the entire world. And as for what you—"

"English Nineteen Fifties Constructivism!"

"What?"

A topic that had come up in a discussion at college. But it checked her.

Then a man came out of the next door shop and said "Molly? What's happening? Is he attacking you?"

"No he is not. It's me attacking him!"

"And if you're not interested in me," said Tommo, "go back now into the shop."

She swivelled, set off, turned back, jerked him up by the collar, said "I texted all my friends and they warned me not to do this!" and marched him to a coffee shop. It was the sort of place that he had always been afraid to enter because people inside looked at him with scorn.

Charlie looked for Shade in the wrecking-pit: reverberation, stamping, arms locked, jostling, knocking over, leather, tattoos, sweaty whooping women, ear, lip, nose, nipple and no doubt cock and labia rings, fuck the no-smoking ban, beards, baldness, guitar howl, spilt beer, blood-thumping percussion. Two old buddies were there but not Shade. Hidden in plain sight, thought Charlie. Some gentleman's fucking club. Getting the smells off himself and putting celery salt on gull's eggs.

Trev, remanded in custody because they wanted to be sure that he had not abducted and abused the children, played draughts with a ram-raider. Off-side front tyre. "Bloody pothole. Puncture. Came to a complete bloody standstill. Local councils. All the bloody money's in their pension funds. Scandal, innit?" The cash machine had been on the back of the pick-up. He pretended that he was a by-stander come to help a stranded driver, but the police hadn't believed him.

"What we reckoned," said Henrietta, "was that you can manage it on the way back from one of those Clerkenwell yuppie furniture jobs."

A mansion flat. Second floor. The sitting room faced north and looked into the trees of the square. It was the studio. Bare boards. Racks. Smell of size. Paint splashes. Old linen tablecloths for curtains. Unshaded bulbs.

"You mean she showed you her studio?" said an amazed Henrietta.

The painter had. She was withheld but amused, and chain smoked and said "You look harassed. I hope it's not me. Have a cup of tea," and the rest of the flat was where she lived, all the doors closed except for the kitchen.

Charlie looked at the stuff on the easels, the same but different portrait, the same but different trees, the same obsession in different lights, and thought 'blimey'.

"We're showing her in Tokyo," said Henrietta, "that's why we needed the drawing."

"Right …" said Charlie. He felt calm as well as unsettled. There had been something about it that could be thought about for a long time.

Later he was in a launderette with the van blankets when Shade texted. Not forgotten. Duty of care. Soon.

"What we must especially beware of," said the woman with multi-coloured spectacle frames, "is prejudice that is so much a part of our received culture that we aren't aware of it, even when we think that we condemn it. Sadly, this contradiction is rife among—" She halted and said "You look interesting. Are you a mature student?"

"I'm the art mover," said Charlie. "Ignore me."

It was a pick-up from another warehouse into which artists had moved while it awaited planning permission. Charlie went to Doris at the far end. She offered a high five and in response to his question about the spectacle frames said "Curator. Michelangelo Prize. Looking for the shock of the new. Cash for the winners."

"Who pays?"

"An oil company. The shortlist's usually anti-capitalist conceptual."

Outside the next space there was a pile of sand atop a glittery frock.

"As this?" said Carlos, who had the bubble and gaffer tape.

"It's called 'Drought'" said Doris. "As in sub-Saharan."

"It was Helmand," said Charlie.

"What?"

A woman in a tinselly head-scarf. They killed her by mistake.

"Nothing," he said.

Doris had a square face and was a posh girl, actually, Sam Howard had explained to Charlie. Single mother. Her chap drowned in a boating accident.

The Curator, narrow jeans tucked into knee boots, trench coat over and an alpaca scarf, nodded at her assistant, who mobile-snapped 'Drought'.

"Water that could save people is polluted by patriarchy-run factories," she said. "More people should be aware of this."

"But where you put the sand?" said Carlos. "In the living room?"

"The cutting edge has moved past ownership," she responded. "Where's the maker?"

Nobody seemed to know.

"In the pub," confided the corner of Doris's mouth to Charlie. "He says he's not interested in celebrity."

Sam Howard, a smiling, awkward, shy man, but stubborn underneath, dealt mostly in hard-edge abstraction, which was hard to sell, so that every time the rent rose he had moved the gallery further east.

He was now on a busy road in Shoreditch, in what had been an ironmongers, and parking was difficult. Charlie pulled out of the traffic into a side street.

"Wait here," he said to Carlos, and strolled back to the gallery.

Outside it a man and woman were arguing.

"You're useless. Absolutely useless. What d'you mean, you don't know what to say?"

"Shut up," said the woman.

"Was he your father or not?"

"When did you care about him, anyway?"

"Oh for God's sake!"

"I want to hit you," said the woman. "I want to smash you in the face!"

131

But it was bluster. She had nowhere to go except the gallery, and went in. The man laughed, lit a cigarette, and stayed outside.

Unsettled, Charlie returned to the van and said "We'll give it half an hour. There's a greasy spoon."

Wrestling posters, formica, sauce bottles, fat sizzle, at one table a black woman with her child in a rickety pushchair, at another building workers with anoraks over grubby white overalls spoke a foreign language. Across the street what had been a greetings-card factory was becoming apartments.

"Can I ask?" said Carlos.

"What?"

"What happen to Ahmed?"

Charlie didn't know.

"People move around. He was an illegal. Squats. Tents. Sleeping rough. A chance of work …". He didn't mention the spooks, and saw that thin, grave Carlos had more on his mind.

"And how's your Mrs Beth?"

He's read me. His banker uncle was kidnapped and shot during the bungled police rescue. This boy's known violence and he knows where I am. He heard himself speak.

"Helping someone. A cousin in Exeter."

"You don't see her?"

Why had he said Exeter?

"I like her," said Carlos. "We all do."

Loud builders' laughter but he did not hear. He spoke but was not sure what. He went outside, realised that he had not paid, gave Carlos a twenty and thought 'Why am I here?' He remembered the gallery and said "There was a couple arguing. It got to me."

*

But they had gone, and Sam was agitated. "Charlie!" he said. "Thank God. Did you see them? What arseholes."

"Who?"

"Alan Gannon's daughter."

"You know them?"

"It's not her. She's just useless. It's her husband."

"The man I saw shouting?"

"If I don't buy in all the work they'll take it somewhere else."

Carlos looked blank. Sam rummaged in a drawer and gave him a catalogue.

"How much do they want?"

"Half a million."

"Can you raise it?"

"Don't be silly."

In the van, traffic clogged around them, Carlos flicked the catalogue. Alan Gannon died of cancer aged 37 when his daughter was two years old. He was successful then forgotten, but students whom he had taught knew how gifted and important he was, and Sam had been one of them. After thirty odd years he heard that the widow had died, went to the daughter, and found the paintings in storage. He mounted an exhibition, sold a couple to the Tate, and rekindled interest. Now the daughter's husband wanted more. He wanted money. He even talked, Sam had said, about showing the paintings more respect.

"Cuidado..!"

Brakes slammed on.

"Sorry," said Charlie.

Horns blared. The girl cyclist they had almost hit kicked their bumper and shouted "Fuck you! Fuck all men!"

*

If she could get to the shop, decided Cindy, she could think it all through and arrive at what's best. She wrote the address down and whenever she felt panic grip her throat looked at what she had written and thought: just miss out what's happened. It was an episode. It's over. Go to the shop. Then home as usual at the end of work. Rosie next door will have picked up the kids. They'll be alone with the telly for one hour max. Then Trev returns or not as the delivery case may be and – she walked against the traffic on the northbound hard shoulder. People hooted. Airstreams wobbled her. A lorry from Romania wanted to pull out, was beeped, swerved back too far and hit her. She was flung twenty feet into concrete banking, and died at once.

"What d'you mean?" said the young woman solicitor assigned to defend him. "You mean they aren't your children at all?"

"No," said Trev.

She gestured.

"It's a fuck-up," said Trev, "Sorry."

"I'm used to it. Just tell me."

She was slim and fair and idealistic, still.

"She had the first kid at sixteen. It meant that she could get a Council flat ..."

"The father?"

"Pick one from five."

"Did she know herself?"

He thought not.

"Is the younger one yours?"

"No, no, she – I'm older than her, you see, and the thing was – I don't know why her family always blamed me but they did, so ..."

He blinked a tear.

"I love them. I love the kids, really. I'm a big kid myself. I love being a spaceman. It's what I imagine when I'm driving, I mean, I'm not ..."

She waited. Her father was a Lord of Appeal and had warned her: you'll be made to realise that for most people there's no longer a framework: no framework to life, I mean: I'm not sure how it happened: is it our fault? I'm not sure.

Wearing what Wendy later described as the wreckage of bespoke tailoring, he came into the shop and said "Package for Charlie March care of the Lady Beth. I hope you don't mind."

"Who are you?"

"Commanding Officer. Duty of care for the men."

My God, she thought. It's that awful Jack Shade.

"D'you mind if I sit down for a minute? I've arranged to be picked up here."

"Picked up..?"

Percy brandished a copy of the next door gallery's catalogue and said "It's what I'd call the integrity end of pot boiling. Impressionist-style depictions of traffic jams. Venice. Nude wives who never age. And so forth. Who's to complain? But that's not what you yourself want to paint, or whatever, is it?"

"Er ..." said Tommo, who had come in with his portfolio.

"Of course, it can take decades to acquire a proper auction value and then if the auction houses set the estimates too high the trade can't bid, which means that in uncertain times the market's fucked when really it isn't, which is ..."

Percy stopped.

"Are those two with you? Don't I recognise the boy?"

Miss Molly and Carlos. Outside. Pretending not to look through the window.

"Er ... he's one of Charlie's ..."

"So he is. And a luscious girl."

"She's mine," blurted Tommo.

"True love?" said Percy. "Fetch them in."

At the door Alastair said "Buenos dias, hombre," to Carlos, and Percy said "This used to be the case, you know. Art students sent to look round the galleries."

"Is no longer?" said Carlos.

"Left wing tutors. Installations. Computer art. Statues of cartoon characters made from factory moulds. Flown everywhere. Taken to Art Fairs in vans with built in showers and loos. In that universe Charlie's a peasant and I'm a dead white man."

In a Saville Row pinstripe, thought Miss Molly, but said nothing.

Alastair had opened the portfolio and Percy flicked an eye without seeming to do so and said "You do realise that this is hopelessly poetically personal and that I can't possibly advance you any money?"

"You mean you like them?" said Miss Molly.

Percy studied her. What awful clothes they wear, he thought. Is it cash that's lacking, or judgement? And he was flattered, and amused, and worried about Charlie, and like some others he'd spoken to thought that Ernest Hannaway had been hard done by.

"Glasses of sherry?" he said. "Or is that – What's the word?"

"Uncool," said Alastair. "I think the glasses might be in the sink."

Piccadilly tube station. One thirty. Lunchtime. And there is something from Shade. Don't look for me, I'll find you. Had said the text. So he stood near the exit that led to the Gents, as though waiting for someone to come up. But one-thirty passed and no-one found him. Should I walk round, he thought, or – Her voice said "Charlie?" He turned.

"Beth? What's …"

He wanted to grab her, and she him, but as people rushed round them neither did.

"Where is Shade?"

She held out a plastic bag. He gripped her hands as she held it and knew that he could not continue without her, and that in the echoing din he was anonymous, and said "Don't you want me to see you naked anymore?"

"I'm not sure. No. I don't know."

"Does it matter?"

"What? No."

"I never thought I'd ask that," he said. "I mean, look at us ..."

Someone carrying a dog almost bumped into her.

"I'll come to you," she said. "Tonight." And scurried to the exit.

Naked beside him after they had made for the first time a floating, gentle sort of love, Beth said "Will we see him again?"

"Mr Shade?"

"Shade."

"I dreamt about him on Monday."

She waited.

"He was in a wood. He recited all the regiment's battle honours and then ..."

"What?"

She was up on her elbow.

"I woke up. He might have shot himself."

"Will he?" she said.

Charlie didn't know. What Shade had sent him in the plastic bag was on the kitchen table. A gold cup. Bacchus and attendants feasting around it. Greek. Buried. Lost. Excavated. Endangered. Looted, smuggled and saved. They weren't sure what to do about it.

Then out of their thoughts Charlie said "Did I ever tell you about the porters in Manchester City Art Gallery?"

"Porters?"

"I was a kid. Me and Mr Macauley. These men in dustcoats were re-hanging."

"Art movers . . ."

"If you like. Anyway, I couldn't resist it and I said 'Excuse me, but what's the heaviest picture you've ever moved?' And this bloke looked at me and said 'Good question. Never forgot it. A Turner. Did my back in but well worth it . . .'"

They laughed. Her mastectomy did not matter, nor the time the oncologist said she had left. All that mattered was the moment.

After

Blood and bowels splashed across my face and clothes, and smoke hid everything, even the enemy, until like lightning inside clouds powder-flashes again exposed shouting men. Held together in the line, left boot behind the next man's right, we urged our horses but they baulked at the pikes. Some of our men were dead but held upright in their saddles by the boot-lock. As we fired and turned to re-load they fell off.

Bullets whistled but other noise seemed distant. We re-locked, everything cumbersome, and went again. Dallison yelled to fire at the centre of the enemy lines, and we did. Horses fell and, smelling the deaths of their kind, others turned. Pikemen were knocked over, and in a jumble Ireton's dragoons were pushed uphill and scattered. We hacked at men on foot and were excited as on firmer ground our mounts quickened, and through dust and kicked-up stones and pieces of turf we came to smokeless sunshine, and shouted and galloped across fields to their baggage wagons, where the guards fired at us, ran, and turned to fire again from a distance.

The camp women were running and some slashed at, breasts split by swords to show their pulpy insides, dresses ripped from the living, the Prince-General pulling up and looking round, and quartermaster Rob Shatterel shouting "Not women! Victuals! We need victuals!"

One guard was still there, with a grin, and someone said "Take off your boots!" and he did, and was kicked and told to go away but drank from a flagon and sat down. I grabbed a ham. I was drunk, I suppose. I suppose most of us were. Then I wanted to piss and dismounted and as I pissed I remembered that I had seen Dallison die, and where was Hart, and was I the one in command now?

Bodies were scattered, not yet stripped, not yet like stiff white muddy sticks. Men still in their saddles drank and threw down empty jars. Dogs ran. We were exhausted and our horses blown and we needed rest.

But a trumpeter blew and the Prince-General was energetic, cuirass over silks, waving his helmet, other officers shouting. Remount. Get back. Get back.

So we learned again what I can repeat these years later, that but for the smoke and the terror, battles would be like the engravings of them: furious huddles with gaps, and some men spectators, even, as we were when we returned too late from our plundering and saw that the cause was defeated.

Cromwell never had lost control of his men and Ireton's had rallied, so that half our people were surrounded and the rest streaming away, ourselves soon among them, the Prince-General's recklessness spent, his arm waving now in resignation, his thoughts regretting, perhaps, as we said among ourselves later, the useless rivalries between himself and the King's other advisers.

And somewhere I had lost my ham and a looted blanket, and it was afternoon and I thought I won't be killed now, and all I want is to hold my love Elizabeth again, and be an actor again, and have lines to learn; and I remembered her laughter when I described those Christmas rehearsals in the Palace itself: the tapestries and paintings, the glow of the brazier, and old Lowin, his breeches down, straining and gasping, but still shouting his dialogue as he sat on the close-stool and shat.

OLD MAN DESPERATION

Most of Wilf's friends from the boozy old amusing showbusiness were dead and only Frank Maguire still telephoned. "You could do e-mail," he said, but Wilf had always written longhand because he believed that if you do not form a word you do not possess it, and so he never mastered typing. Frank's plays were still performed sometimes, but Wilf had never secured a comparable reputation. He had successes but they were never at the centre of anyone's interest. His proper subject-matter was his family and the cotton towns but for some reason he had blocked it, made excuses, and said to himself that he would write it when he had resolved other matters.

Even so, Frank Maguire had always felt that Wilf had the greater natural gift. He respected Wilf's education and his judgement. Most people compromised or fudged their opinions. Wilf did not. Wilf was vain but amusing, shy but outspoken.

Frank the son of a factory hand thought that it had been easier for himself to be free than it had for Wilf the son of a mill manager: easier to shed inhibitions, easier to forgive, easier to please other people and easier to realise that life changes around us but we do not notice.

Then fifteen years ago – or was it twenty? – had come the events that defined Wilf as out of date.

He pitched his Sleep-Out idea to a TV producer friend who said "I've no muscle anymore. I'm on the way out. Things aren't what they were …"

Well, Wilf had thought, you always did drink too much, and that explains it.

But it didn't, Frank had known, and tried to elaborate and say "What do you expect?" but to little avail.

Then Wilf got a stage play on but had written it badly, and a radio project came to nothing. The new person in his agent's office said that current executive thinking in television was that people of Wilf's generation had lost touch with the audience.

"But they should know who I am, for fuck's sake!" Wilf replied, and hung up. Old man desperation, thought the person in the office. It doesn't work for me.

By then Wilf had moved to the Island. He still wrote but did not try to sell anything. He doesn't want rejection by stupid people, thought Frank, and at this stage I don't blame him. Then Frances died. Wilf was marooned, as it were, living in the town but not quite a part of it.

He saw weekender friends, most made by Frances, and went to

slide talks at the Historical Society. He would sit at the back and at the end slip away. When he still drove a car he went to beaches and stared at the waves. Sometimes he went to the mainland and stayed at a hotel, to show that he still could; or visited a gallery, as he and Frances had once done in London and Paris and Amsterdam and Italy.

Is it a defect that I don't much need other people, or is that what happens to writers? Who cares? What I need to explain is changes to the world.

And now he was old and in the middle of a summer night woke up unable to breathe. The doctor said that it had been a heart attack and that he'd arrange an ECG. Keep writing, thought Wilf. I must keep writing.

NICOLAS BURT

Our infantry had been destroyed, our materiel abandoned or captured: wagons, remnants, wives, camp-boys, beef on the hoof, gunpowder, the King's coach and his private papers. We drifted westwards from Naseby. The war, we knew, was decided but not ended. This or that would happen, said rumours. The roads were unrepaired, crops commandeered or ruined, upkeep neglected. People were weary and suspicious. Every day dozens of men deserted. We discussed it but decided that we could not. We were still actors of the King's Company, and he was at Oxford, and so for all we knew were our senior colleagues Mr Lowin and Mr Taylor. What if there were peace talks, and while they were in progress we were called upon to play?

At eighteen Wilf's carer April had won a place at university. The teachers were chuffed. If she finds the right middle-class boyfriend, opined Mr Wilson, she could get herself out of the usual mess and be somebody. Science Teacher Mrs Hopkins thought this ridiculously sexist, and said so, but at the same time had to admit that a man does change a woman, as she had experienced herself and still puzzled over.

Then April, pert-bottomed, quick-witted, eager to be out in the world and confident that she could crack it whatever it was, took a gap year job on the mainland but fell pregnant, and was not sure by whom or which. She returned to the Island, was defended by her mother, and decided to skip university and keep the baby.

"Catastrophic," said Mr Wilson when he heard about it. "Why do we bother?"

Bother or not, April got on with her life. There was one sort of job or another, a second son by another casual father, and a stroke of luck when she secured a long-term lease on her flat. She always attracted men but never needed them to be with her for long. She pursued internet conspiracy theories with vigour and realised one day that she was thirty-seven, and ought to be more secure. So she qualified as a carer, was taken on by an agency, and for the flexibility opted to help people who still lived in their homes.

One of the first was the old schoolteacher Mr Wilson, who was not surprised when April said that she believed in Aliens. He had maggots teeming in his ulcer, and another client had forgotten her own name but remembered wartime bombing, and sometimes smeared excrement across her wallpaper.

April could cope, and saw herself as battling for them all. Wilf's medication seemed to have contained his heart leak, but he became a client after his fall when carrying fire logs. April was amused by him. He eyed her body in a way that implied what might have occurred had the disparity in their ages been different, lent her books, and had funny stories about other worlds.

On the other hand he could be uncooperative, and made outrageous remarks about what was on television and political correctness, and asked questions such as "What would it be like, a world with which women were satisfied?". Social Services considered him a menace to himself, and were not keen to help. If he sold up he could pay for himself to be in a private home, they thought, and public money spent on someone with none.

"That's how they are, of course," said April's Manager, who saw herself as despite all the blows she had received a cheerful realist. "Leftie soak-the-rich do-gooders."

"Should you be saying that?"

"No. But how would your Wilf go in a Care Home?"

"He'd disintegrate," said April. "It'd kill him."

"You mean you suspect he's got dementia as well?"

"I did e-mail that M.P. woman," said April, "but she never replied."

NICHOLAS BURT

We were the Prince-General's lifeguard, and when he surrendered Bristol we were allowed to keep our carbines, and escorted part of the way to Oxford by Parliamentary cavalry. Their leaders Fairfax and Cromwell rode beside the Prince-General, and hob-nobbed. Then they bade us a civil farewell and seemed as sad as we were, and as anxious for a resolution. Cromwell wore a rough scarf for the autumn but despite the frosts Oxford seemed out of any season or good sense.

Our actor colleagues had left, although there were still some musicians and Court ladies. We were quartered in College rooms that seemed to have been ransacked, and staked our horses in the quadrangle. Townspeople were sullen, yet the King walked his dogs as though nothing had happened. Then on the second day he released us.

"Until London," said a chamberlain, "and plays in the Palace again!"

But we were apprehensive and as after dark we ate fritters in an inn stable, Rob Shatterel said "What was that line you said in that play you were in?".

Charlie Hart looked up, the neat leading-man shape of him, the eyes that to this day you can read no matter where you stand or sit. He tried to smile, and said "I am Duchess of Malfi still ..."

GENERAL ELECTION

April drove Wilf to the Polling Station that was in the Council offices on a bluff overlooking the bay. The wind buffeted and rain spattered. Inside, photo blow-ups of the town in its Victorian resort heyday adorned the walls of the rooms that had been cleared, and election furniture installed. The queue was of mostly older people and the Presiding Officer and two Clerks were very serious. I hope to goodness he remembered who he wanted to vote for, thought April. Then she spoiled her own ballot by writing FREE SANITARY PRODUCTS FOR WOMEN across it, and drove him home.

The sky lifted and wet surfaces gleamed. Around the house the evergreens were a dripping mess and gutters leaked. There were eaves, turrets, stained glass, six bedrooms and a conservatory. Hadn't it been a B and B once?

But how much would repairs cost, wondered April, and were they worth it?

"Impulse buy," Wilf would say. "My one and only sale of film rights. Frances wanted something by the sea ..."

Frances. Twenty years his junior and dead now of the embolism.

"Tuna sandwich?" said April. "Mustard in the salad cream?"

After she left Wilf tried to write, but there was the ache behind his forehead again, and a blank when he sought a situation that would be the metaphor for what he wanted to show. So he again told himself aloud what he had witnessed but did not seem able to pass on as a story.

The phone rang but this time he ignored it. When April arrived next morning he was in his underpants and a scarf and swearing at the television.

"Look at them. Bloody newsreaders. All they do is read autocues but they think they're philosopher kings."

The conservatory table was strewn with noteboooks and files.

"Did you fetch these from upstairs?" said April.

His bed was downstairs, as was the shower room. He was supposed never to go upstairs when alone.

"It's my Sleep Out idea. It's like the bloody Attlee Government ..."

Don't, she thought. I could repeat the rest myself. All the money spent on welfare and no attention paid to industrial decline. Later they abolished Grammar schools and skewed the curriculum and –

"It obsesses me," he said.

"What obsesses me is that you could have another fall and then what?"

Why can't she see that what I've got to do is keep on writing?

"Anyway. Boris won. So what you wanted happened. Are you warm enough? Have you had a shower yet?"

He tapped his chest. Short breath again. Give us a moment. She did. After the shower he dressed, and she made toast.

"What happened to your Mary, by the way?"

"What?"

Mary. Tory Remainer. Member of Parliament. Bustling, buxom and bossy. Wilf's cousin at one remove. Her grandmother Beatrice had been Wilf's mother's sister, but the two fell out because Beatrice had fancied Wilf's father first.

"Oh. Yes. Well. She wasn't standing, was she?"

"But I thought you said …"

"Don't you remember? De-selected. Booted out. What else did she expect? Stupid, screeching …"

"Will you call her?"

Call her? He hadn't spoken to her since that ridiculous funeral ten years ago.

"What I need," he said, "is a writing plan."

They're your only blood people, thought April. We need to know. Will they want to help when you get worse?

DOLLY SWEEP

When Mr Lowin came back from Oxford I was – Well I'm not sure how old I was because I was found under a hedge by a bird-catcher, who gave me to the honeywoman who – Not true. I was found here in Brentford, in a basket on the mud-flats at mid-tide, and someone said "Look at her robe. She's a rich woman's love-child abandoned." Was that true? What did the wild geese say? They said "Give her to that skivvy at The Three Pigeons. Her bastard was stillborn so she still has the milk in her breasts …"

Which is how I became a skivvy, and because Brentford was famous for your follow-me-whatnot, Mr Lowin bought The Three Pigeons with his theatre money, and didn't Mr Jonson mention it in his play? He did, and what used to happen, what you'd do if you were a gallant or just a silly old man with some money was that you'd have a few early noggins at The Chequer at

Queenhythe, and then take a boat up-river with your fancy woman and land at Brentford pier, where there were fiddlers who'd play you ashore and ask for five shillings.

They were a nuisance, actually, and in another play didn't Mr Massinger have one of his characters complain about them? He did. "Cannot the shaking of the sheets be danced without your piping?" he wrote.

The shaking of the sheets. When Mr Lowin told me that he said "Should I be discussing saucy meanings with a girl your age?" and I said "Too late to stop now, Mr Lowin ..."

Which was all before the War, and on the day he returned by boat from Oxford he was very old and short of breath and with little more than he sat slumped in, really. He looked at the mess of what had been his goldmine and said "Can you fetch me a strong water?" and we had to explain.

Soldiers had smashed and stolen everything, all strong waters, other spirits and wine, and all we could afford were local ale and beer brewed without hops. Mr Lowin, always a big awkward man, said "Ale then, and give us a song ..."

> Oh I heard a bird that sat in a tree
> And sang look at me look at me
>
> And I saw an actor up on the stage
> Who sang look at me look at me
>
> And I am the skivvy who sweeps the floor
> And sings pity me pity me
>
> And I loved a—

I stopped because Mr Lowin blinked tears, but more of anger than sorrow. "All that world," he said, "all that bloody wonderful world. Who else is still here with you?"

I told him. Mother Gossip and Old Ralph. Oh, and two

discharged soldiers slept upstairs. They'd nowhere to go. And there was money owed but no July cattle fair and no pleasure trade.

"All of which is why we can't yield!" he boomed in his old voice. Someone once said that you could hear him even if you were in the street outside the theatre, but when I asked him about that he said he'd never overacted in his life. He'd left that to the windfuckers at the Red Bull and the Fortune.

Old Ralph appeared. He held a chicken by its legs.

"I've rung him neck," he said. "I'll roast him with nettles and chestnuts."

COOKIE

Spring was delayed by weeks of rain. Dead leaves lingered. A garden seat had fallen apart. Spiders. Are there cobwebs over the upstairs furniture, Wilf wondered. Are there moths? If I touched my dinner jacket would it come to pieces? Dinner jacket? You had a dinner jacket? I did. Awards Ceremony, Café Royal. We didn't win. There were brittle gilt dining chairs and one or two drunks lay among them. In the lift afterwards I met – Blank. Famous actor. He looked like Nosferatu, and why did I just answer the land line? I said "Yes?" and whoever it was said "Mr Wilfred?" and babble, babble, babble another bloody cold call. Double-glazing but not pronouncing the 'G' at the end. Frank's not called for weeks and I've not called Johnny Derker for months and I'm on gravel in my stockinged feet and –

An anxious and beautiful young woman was at the gate, under the sodden macrocarpa. How like her, he thought. She's refused to be old.

He mumbled.

"What?"

A nickname.

Oh, no. Fuck no. He thinks I'm his wife. She saw what a jumble his clothes were, and the collapsed curtains at one of the windows.

"But you're dead, aren't you? Didn't they say? Aren't you?"

"I must have thought I'd give you a surprise."

"Snappy dialogue," said Wilf. "Very good."

He knew who she was now and thought: how can I be in this mess? I'm old. I don't need mess.

"Sorry," she said. "You've not seen me for ten years so why would you—"

"Cookie," he said. "Did Mary send you?"

"I've not seen any of them for months."

Awkwardness. So why are you here? So now that I am are you asking me in or what?

"Actually," said Wilf, "I'm not sure where the coffee tin is."

FALCON STAIRS

Then I went to London with Mr Lowin, but by accident. I carried his bundle to the boat and got in myself, so that me and the boatman could each hold one of Mr Lowin's hands to help him. But no sooner done, and him settled under the tilt, than the boatman's boy shoved off and the tide took us, and I couldn't get back to the steps.

"Dolly what is it about you and daft things on this river?"

"Rhymes," I said.

> Riddle me river, riddle me re
> Mortlake and mallards and swans one two three
> Mr Lowin and Dolly sail down to the sea

"We aren't bound for the sea," he retorted. "Find a rhyme for Falcon Stairs."

"Roof repairs," I said, and snowflakes began, and whirled all the way, and at London itself the sky was darker because of the smoke, and the buildings looked glum and huddled up for comfort. On the Southwark side the stairs jutted over mudflats, and they were named for falcons because people flew their birds from the marshy fields, said Mr Lowin as we trudged across them to his house in Maiden Lane.

When we were almost there he stopped and pointed. "See this building site? It's where our Globe Theatre was pulled down …"

WHY HAVE YOU COME?

Inside Wilf asked about the journey. Had she come from London? More or less. Was the hydrofoil crowded? Were people on the mainland worried about the pandemic? She gave him the coffee tin. Her phone pinged.

"The famous social media," he said, "that was supposed to set us free. Like the famous Nineteen Sixties."

"Sod off!" she said.

"What?"

"Not you. This gaslighter …"

"Come to think of it," said Wilf, "you wrote that play, didn't you? Edinburgh Fringe etfuckingcetera …"

His grin, she thought, that she had heard them talk about.

What day of the week is it, thought Wilf, for no reason at all. Why can't I stop that dribble of piss before I lift the seat?

Doors opened and April came in. They all stared. The kettled steamed.

Wilf said "This is Cookie. Mary's daughter. She hasn't said yet why she's come."

In London we found fortune good and bad. The good was a house that belonged to the Cumbrian family of an officer we knew from Oxford. They owned lead mines and to promote this interest among financiers had bought in Covent Garden, new-built and fashionable. So had many similar people but the War emptied the area. No Court seasons or meaningful Legal Terms. No luxury trades. Our friend had given us a letter to the lawyer who held the house keys and we found damp and cobwebs as well as comforts beyond those of the lodgings and taverns and whorehouses we had known. Then within days Charlie had to rescue me from drink and bad places in Turnbull Street.

My Elizabeth's mother had never warmed to me, nor I to her. An actor was not in her opinion a good match for the daughter of a master combmaker. Throughout the War I had contrived to send messages and tokens from Oxford to London but if they arrived at all they had been interrupted, we came to suppose, by Elizabeth's mother, and Elizabeth herself allowed to think that I had been killed in a skirmish.

So she married a Dutch merchant and went to Amsterdam, where people are more sympathetic to the pure religion, said the combmaker's man sent to turn me away from the doorstep.

Charlie found me a while later in Turnbull Street and said "Shake yourself. Come on. Come on." We had sold our horses but the money would not last long. We needed work, if there was any. We discovered that although the City authorities had shut all theatres for the duration some people were giving sneak performances. Actors we knew drank in The Fleece, or The Rose in Russell Street, and Charlie and Rob had already talked to them. The word was, they said, that old Lowin had returned.

THE ROMAN EMPIRE

They sat with coffees at the kitchen table. She'd come on an impulse, said Cookie. Spur of the moment. She'd heard so much talk about Wilf that she wanted to – well – you know. Find out what he's really like.

But she looked elsewhere and April thought: this is wrong. This is not the entire story. Be careful.

"I did e-mail your mother. Some while ago. Did you know?"

"If you sent it to her office ..." said Cookie, with an airy gesture ... "Blown away. De-selection." And with a twisty smile ... "Political fall-out."

That could be true, realised April.

"Anyway, now that you are here, it could really help with Wilf's situation. Don't we feel?"

No response from either.

"I don't want you to say anything that's not my business, so don't think ..."

"What she probably thinks," said Wilf, "is that women in the Senate would have prevented the fall of the Roman Empire."

"What?"

"Ignore him," said April. "He should be cancelled."

"I have been. So you're safe to stay. Back bedroom."

"Er ... I'll show her where everything is," said April.

LONDON BRIDGE

To save boat money we walked. The wind blew the stink of the Fleet Ditch tanneries, and on London Bridge itself half the shops were boarded up. Then as we came to the Southwark end Charlie stopped.

"What?"

A man we recognised had come with a companion from the Bear Tavern.

"My oath!"

"Yes."

"Ellyart Swanston."

"They say he's begun life again," said Charlie, "as a goldsmith."

Ellyart Swanston was the only London actor, so far as anyone knew, to have joined the army of the Parliament, and there were many harsh words that we had wanted to say to him. Yet he had been a shareholder in the King's Company, and the person who recommended me to them, and I was glad to see him, and he us, as he cracked his knowing grin and spread his cloak like wings to welcome us.

"Well met, lads," he cried, "and providential!"

Charlie's laugh spluttered, and I know why. Mr Swanston always had a scheme afoot. It was he, after all, who had handled the wartime sales, of the Globe to the property projectors, and of the company's costumes and stage effects to the four winds. At the same time, and always somehow a friend to all sides, he had ensured that Mrs Lowin and Mrs Taylor, struggling in London when their men were in Oxford, received their share of the moneys.

"Still conniving, are we?" I could not help saying, even if he was my senior and I should have deferred.

"Well spotted," he chuckled, "and if it's old Lowin you seek, so do we!"

His eyes were shifty-small, and those of his companion appraising.

*

HELP LINE

They bickered all day without either of them coming to what both knew to be the point. For dinner they had macaroni cheese from the freezer. Cookie roamed, looking for something but not saying what. Eventually she lolled on the sofa and rolled a joint. She blew the smoke at Wilf as he watched the television. It was an episode of an in-fashion crime series set on the South Coast. At the end a caption and voice-over said that if viewers were affected by any of the issues raised in the programme there was a Help Line.

Before Cookie could stop him Wilf, who had muttered throughout, was dialling.

"Yes," he said, as someone answered. "Thank you. You can help me. What? Well – I'm in my late eighties. I have suspected early dementia and a heart condition, and I experience shortness of breath when – What? No. Over-acting. Having to watch naff dialogue and over-acting causes me physical and particularly profound mental distress, and—"

A mollifying tone, as though to a child.

Wilf asked if any of the self-righteous wanking do-gooders running British television had any artistic rigour at all, and was cut off.

Cookie threw a cushion at him. He laughed. She called him names and stomped upstairs.

LEATHER COAT

Well. I answered the door and it wasn't so much being knocked down by a feather as by an entire smirking bolster as this pleased-with-himself man cried "You must be that water-sprite

Dolly Sweep of whom we've heard!" and without waiting for a curtsey bundled in, kissed Mrs Lowin's hand, said "Bumped into these lads on the Bridge, John!" and threw more wood on the fire.

One of 'these lads', Mr Burt as I discovered, had a black eye and the other was Mr Charlie. He was the more comely, as ladies who read poetry say, and behind them was a man in a long leather coat. He was the sort that says nothing but you remember him, and I did.

Mrs Lowin mouthed "Ale with herbs!" at me and they all laughed and back-slapped and talked at once except for Mr Burt, who was sorry for himself, and the man in the leather coat who sat down. But Mrs Lowin said "My word! Not Mr Moseley, is it? Not after all these months?"

At which I knew something was afoot because I'd seen your Mr Moseley three days ago in the street with Mr Lowin and as I stared with my mouth open the bolster-man they called Mr Swanston said "Taylor's back from Oxford, I hear, but with a rheum …"

"Well," said Mr Lowin. "Are you surprised? It's his old habits. Always pausing to make his effect. Always having a doubt and always, or I'm a fanfaroon, the most stupendous breaker of wind on the English stage!"

Mr Swanston and the lads were delighted.

"The leading player of the King's Company," went on Mr Lowin, "and on he comes. If music be the food of love, play on …"

He made a loud farting noise. Strewth, I thought.

"Unbelievable. Why did audiences never clock it?"

There was a big discussion as to why. I loved it.

"I want to be an actor," I said. "I want to go on and fart."

They stared.

"You can't read or write," said Mr Lowin. "So how could you learn to break wind?"

"I'll teach her reading," said Mrs Lowin. "An hour a day, bright and early."

They all wanted their say about this, and it gave Mr Swanston the chance to come to the point.

"Speaking of acting," he said, "when will you venture a return to it?"

Well. They were at the King's command but the King wasn't here and they'd no theatre of their own and some were very rheumaticky and too old to dance in hell, or in prison for that matter, and – Well, said Mr Swanston, who had his acquaintances everywhere, the City authorities are in several minds at once as to who they should try to please. So they turn a blind eye now but will they do so for ever, and in the meantime, to speak bluntly, you're not making any money are you?

No. They were not.

"Not that I'm one of the Company any more," said Mr Swanston, "except that in law and friendship I'm still a shareholder, and we still own the playbooks, don't we?"

Mr Charlie clicked his fingers. So that's it!

Mr Swanston made a flourish and gestured, so that we all looked at quiet Mr Moseley, who stayed sitting, cleared his throat, and made his offer.

CIGGIES

What it was like, said April when she reported to her Manager, was the jungle when gorillas rush about and screech at each other.

"Wilf didn't rush about, surely?"

Cookie had done enough for the pair of them. She forgot things. Went back. Stuffed them in her haversack. Imprecated over Wilf's shouts.

"If only transgenders play transgenders I suppose only serial killers will play serial killers?" Wilf mocked.

"You're rancid and don't even notice it!"

"Stop it! Wilf! Both of you! Why are you doing this?"

When the gorillas screech, suggested April's Manager, isn't it about sexual dominance?

"What?"

"He won't interfere with her, will he?"

April surprised herself.

"Well, it is like sex going wrong," she said, "but it's about something else ..."

Her Manager, divorced after all from a vicar who ran off with a parishioner, had seen more of it than most.

"So what did you do?" she said.

Remembered an Agency rule: if you smoke never do so in front of a client. So she grabbed Cookie's elbow and said "Outside for a ciggie!"

"Get off me!"

"Outside..!"

As they went she made her point. "I'm responsible for this old man however annoying he is, and ..."

On the gravel Cookie shrugged her off. But she did listen. Okay. Okay. Then she half-laughed at herself.

She's ripe, thought April. She's young and juicy in the way that I'm not anymore. She lit up and blew out.

"I've sussed you, you know," said Cookie. "Awesome. You're actually a sort of free woman, aren't you?"

"You can be," said April, "when you live in a place that doesn't matter to anyone."

Crikey, thought Cookie. "Give us a drag," she said, took one, and coughed.

"Hoped it might be dope?"

"Wilf uses gluten-free as an insult ..."

"Wilf wants to make you think. Tell me why you came."

Cookie pulled a leaf from a bush. "I found my girl-friend in bed with a man. Went ballistic."

"But why come here?"

Another shrug. Then she pointed. A red squirrel foraging upside-down.

"Wow ...!"

It scampered away.

"Cookie ..." persisted April.

"Home isn't home."

April waited.

"They don't exactly want me to be what I am."

"What's that to do with Wilf?"

A dismissive gesture.

"Maybe it's better if I forget it. Better if I do fuck off, actually."

Inside, when they told Wilf, he waved the remote at the television and said "Too late. You can't."

"What?"

The pandemic. Government action. Lockdown.

Why am I surprised? thought April. This room is always unreal. The gloom and then the conservatory. It's like being inside a light bulb.

INK SPIDER

"We live," said Mr Moseley, "in slippery times, in which the slightest pamphlet is more vendible than the works of the learnedest man ..." and he made it seem not so much an opinion as a discovery, not a criticism of strident ignorance but an amazement that so much of it existed. And indeed, in those days there did seem to be more hectoring pamphlets than arses to be wiped on them, and when Dolly Sweep used our privy she said that there were so many folio sheets that it was like sitting in a pile of autumn leaves and where were the paper lice?

"Very good," said Charlie. "Wood lice. Paper lice. Very good."

"All eaten by ink spiders, d'you reckon?" said Dolly, and being used by now to Mr Moseley's pretended spectatorship of events of which he was the prime mover, we obeyed the summons to his printing shop, enjoyed his Umble Pies and hot ale with sugar, apples and spices and waited to hear what he wanted from us.

His offer, which Mr Lowin accepted, had been to publish a Folio Edition of Comedies and Tragedies by Mr Beaumont and Mr Fletcher. But he needed our help, he said.

In the piping days of peace, he explained, it had taken about a month from receiving a play text to its publication as an unbound folio. Subscribed or subsequently ordered bound copies would need longer. Now, as we could see, he had lost one apprentice to the Army and another to the gunpowder factory, where wages were high even though, as he understood it, Parliament was strapped for cash and arrears frequent.

And in this Beaumont and Fletcher instance, he continued, we had not one play to publish but at the final count twenty-nine. The time this would take to assemble, type-set and print we could calculate for ourselves. So could me and Charlie assist? We were acquainted with playscripts after all, and by his own admission the eyesight of Mr Knight, the Company's long-standing Book Holder, was failing. We would of course receive what would, alas, be not much more than token stipends. Nevertheless—

CLOTHES

"But she could have left," said April's Manager. "She could have gone home or wherever and self-isolated."

Self-isolation, Wilf had observed, was what writers sought above all, but for the most part the world denied them.

Cookie had smiled at this.

"See?" said Wilf, "She's not self-declared Triple Binary at all. She's one of us."

Cookie showed him the finger, at which he put out his tongue.

"So they're actually like kids with each other," said April's Manager.

"Anyway," said Cookie, "how can I stay? I've no clothes."

"In the wardrobes," said Wilf. "Hanger after hanger. Drawer after drawer."

They had belonged to Frances. April had asked him why he never disposed of them. "They remind me," he said, "and they're beautiful."

"They're not girly, are they?" demanded Cookie. "I don't do girly."

"Why not try a few?" said April.

"Did she?" said April's Manager. "How did she look in them?"

Great. She knew all about them. Who designed them. How much they had cost when they were new. How much they would fetch if Wilf sold them.

"So much for not doing girly..."

"There's this older woman who wants to marry her," explained April.

Imagine telling your mother that. Come to it, imagine yourself as the mother.

As Cookie swished a skirt at the mirror April said "What do you actually want? To stay or to go?"

"I want to go. But not until I've found out what I want to know."

"What's that?"

Cookie told her. Unbelievable, thought April. Or is it?

"So why don't we go down now," she said, "and ask him?"

*

PAPERS FOUL AND FAIR

The scripts that writers delivered to a theatrical company were in their own handwriting and called Foul Papers. Sometimes collaborators would write alternate scenes, or one the serious plot-line and the other the comic, and occasionally a third man would be called in to enliven a particular speech. The Company's Book Keeper, or one of his scribes, would make from these papers a copy of the entire play that was called Fair, the dialogue in Secretary Hand and the directions in Italic.

These first copies were submitted to the Censor and returned, often with comments and required amendments scrawled over, and when the text was settled the Book-Keeper would supervise the sheets for the actual production of the play: the Scenario of Acts, Scenes, Properties and Effects, which would be pinned up in the Tiring House, and each actor's individual Part (or Parts) with his Cues and Exits.

When we knew our lines we would return these Part Books to the Book-Keeper. Scenes in which we did not appear we did not receive in writing, and so we never knew the whole play until we heard it in rehearsal.

What Mr Moseley, reckoned, and he was right, was that what me and Charlie were used to as actors would make it easier to assemble in the printing shop those plays of which the complete copies had been lost, or had suffered foul or missing pages.

And, well – we needed the money and we enjoyed the work. Sometimes we pieced together scenes in which one or both of us had acted and the Master Printer and the remaining apprentice laughed with us at our memories. My self-esteem mended (foolishly I suppose, now) because my Secretary Hand was better than Charlie's, although he was the more adept typesetter, and Mrs Moseley grew flowers and herbs in the yard, there were hens and pigs in an outhouse, the skivvy would be sent down with nettle soup and we knew the street fish sellers and hawkers and threw snowballs with the local urchins.

Then, one frosty day after Christmas, when we had proofs and the first Subscription Copies were already at the Binders, old Josh who sang and sold street ballads clattered in and said had we heard the news?

The King, who had gone to the Scots in the hope that their army would support him, had again played too many tricks. The Scots had abandoned him and he was a prisoner of Fairfax and Cromwell and the Army, which was a-boil with agitators and wild preachers, and what did this turn of events mean?

If the Generals had taken more power would men who now had less alter their opinions to suit? Men, we meant, such as those who at Stationer's Hall licensed the printing of books.

In the workshop we feared the worst. Mr Beaumont and Mr Fletcher had written some things that seemed to criticize royal policies. At the same time they had made most of their living from the King's patronage of our Company. Pamphleteers, preachers and common soldiers now questioned such niceties, and called them hypocrisy. Would Stationer's Hall concur, and deny publication?

We should have known better than to ask. Mr Moseley's footwork, in that world he called slippery, was impeccable. He had long secured permission to dedicate the book to Lord Herbert, a staunch opponent of the King, and persuaded writers of differing opinions to pen introductory laudations; and besides, he always knew from his man among them how opinion went among the more radical merchants and minor office-holders.

That man, of course, was Mr Swanston, who considered himself the angler but was in truth a fish. So the Folio Edition was published, in that February of 1647, to both acclaim and profit.

*

April's Manager stirred a fourth spoonful of sugar into her tea (thinking 'I must cut down on this, but on the other hand I haven't had any ice cream for nine days') and said "Good tactics. So downstairs again? What happened?"

The phone had rung. No-one responded. Then April did.

"It's Frank Maguire ..." she mouthed.

Wilf gestured. Not me. Not now.

Okay. Okay.

Cookie looked from one to the other.

April returned.

"Frank said to tell you that old Ernie died, but Viv's okay and sends her love. She's had Ernie's old gallery come back to her, Frank said, but she told them to piss off. Does that make sense?"

"All too much," said Wilf.

"Who's Ernie?" said Cookie.

Wilf said "A painter. He did that abstract on the wall behind you."

Pictures and things fascinated her, but she did not know enough about them, and had not asked.

We were young, said Wilf, and we squatted in this mansion flat and Ernie played Wagner so loudly that when the Gods crossed into Valhalla you could have been on the bridge with them. So they called it Valhalla and –

"Is that the Frank Maguire who wrote—"

"Marvellous. You've heard of him."

"He was a set book."

Wilf supposed he was, and anyway Ernie's paint cans had been everywhere and Viv walked around topless and there was that smart but dodgy – Then he stopped.

"Smart but dodgy?"

"I forget. At least, I think it was Viv. What's that line in 'Paradise Lost'?"

166

April had never heard of 'Paradise Lost' but Cookie said "Justify the ways of God to Man?"

"No," said Wilf.

But they grinned at each other, like equals, and April saw a change in Cookie, and a decision to postpone her question.

Be patient, she thought, and said "Come on. I'll cut your toenails."

As she removed his socks Wilf remembered the lines:

> Methought I saw my late espoused Saint
> Brought to me like Alcestis from the grave

Except that it wasn't 'Paradise Lost'. And it wasn't Viv that he remembered.

D-O-L-L-Y

C-A-T cat. D-O-G-G-E dogge. E-N-U-F-F enough. No. Sorry. What I mean is that the day I spelled P-H-Y-S-I-C-K-E physicke rite (Sorry. Right.) for the first time, at which Mrs Lowin was very pleased with me, there was an occurrence on the street we called Long Southwark. Samuel How the cobbler, a very quiet man but of a sudden possessed and shouting, saw Jesus enter the pie-shop on the corner, and began to preach, and people of all sorts to listen. Wild questions like those in the pamphlets we wiped ourselves on. Who is the Chief Leveller? Jesus Christ. He is the Chief Leveller. It's thunder and lightning coming, said Mrs Lowin. Mark my words.

HANG-GLIDING

I could die this afternoon, thought Wilf, or in bed tonight, and who would care or remember? The ironing lady did not appear, nor the cleaner, nor the occasional gardener. April went from one client's crisis to another. Young people were demoralised by the lockdown. Mothers hated being stuck with children. Serve them right, thought Wilf. No fortitude. How could they have? Cocaine dinner parties blaming knife crime on funding cuts. Fast fashion. Cheap flights. Decades of daft dreams and – Why am I so angry? Why do I say stupid unkind things to people? The postman. I was outside. He came through the gate. We kept a Covid distance. He said "I like that scarf you're wearing. Very flamboyant." I replied "Well. It's Hermes, isn't it?" Which it wasn't. So why did I say that? Why? Why did I show off in that way? Have I always been stupid? Have I always – Yes, I suppose I – He walked.

Out of the house and down the hill. Into the town. Everything was silent. No people. Carried off, he imagined, by Algerian corsairs. They'll appear in the slave market.

Jarvis the window cleaner was up a ladder and said "Wilf ? What are you doing?"

"Hang-gliding," said Wilf.

Jarvis put him in the van and drove him back.

There was this girl. Slender. Agitated. Luscious hair. She'd phoned the police. Then April arrived. Her secret smile, despite everything, for Jarvis. They had been at school together. She was canny even then and he knew not to rush her. Her women friends said was it true that he had an anchor tattooed on each buttock?

"Where were you going?" April asked Wilf. "What did you want?"

"I suppose," he said, "that I was trying to fly away from myself."

COVENT GARDEN

Then no work and months of gloom. We felt useless. Preachers shouted. The King was not to be trusted but what could replace him? Prostitutes hugged us and said we could pay later, but we felt stupid afterwards. Then on a grey sweltering summer day the Army leaders acted and entered London itself. The urine from their horses, and the kites that wing-clattered in the confusion to peck at the dung. The din as troopers smashed open doors and installed themselves in empty houses. Covent Garden.

THE DAYLIGHT FOX

Then the cleaning lady appeared and said sorry but she really needed the money and was that okay? Wilf said "It's better than okay. It's terrific." So they left her to it, Cookie upstairs and Wilf in the garden with a scarf, his green and yellow one. He felt better. He took deep breaths, closed his eyes, and tried to empty his mind. When he looked again a fox had come from the bushes. It stopped in front of him and on its haunches spoke wise words. Then it trotted away.

DOLLY AT THE FORTUNE THEATRE

Prithee, winter, do not snow! Do not snow, prithee! Which it didn't but it was nose-nip cold and coaches blocked the streets, drivers swore, gutters were ice, horses blew and wives in furs had to get out and (oops!) walk. But hadn't they clenched their buttocks for months for a chance to go out and flaunt, and hadn't – Oh, and there were hot pie stalls and stilt-walkers and musicians ("No alteration there, then," said Mr Lowin, "still their hideous drum and trumpet acting!") and never mind the giddy noise, what shape-shifted me was when everyone hushed to listen and even the actor held his breath at what might happen. "A leaf from Mr Taylor's book of dramatic pauses," said Mr Lowin, but I thought I'd tumble from the overhang and float into paradise and ever afterwards and for all my life be –

"Well. It was your first time at the theatre," smiled Mrs Lowin.

"Pre-War prices again?" asked Mr Lowin.

Mr Burt nodded. A penny. Another for the galleries, and another for the cushioned seats.

"This is what I've been saying," said Mr Lowin. "We must play indoors and charge more."

"It was full," said Mr Hart.

"We need a bigger take," insisted Mr Lowin. "We need enough to see us through until we're back to normal …"

Even Mr Swanston had stopped saying when that might be. But he had invested in sea-coal, and sent us half a load.

GORGEOUS KNICKERS

Wilf waited until April arrived to take his blood pressure. The balloon on his arm tightened, hurt him, deflated. April studied the read-out.

"It's all over the place again," she said.

"Well," he said, "I did have this conversation with a fox …"

They stared at him.

"A dog," asked Cookie, "or a vixen?"

"A dog. An old one. For the road."

"What did he say?"

"He said that firstly, despite whatever else may be going on, we should tell your father and mother and brothers—"

"Who don't give a toss."

"—where you are, and—"

Cookie sputtered random annoyance. They were at odds among themselves. All they care about is – When she walked out what did they do? They went to Paris and they wouldn't care if Cookie jumped into the Danube and as for—

"The Danube?"

"Oh shut up!"

"And secondly," Wilf persisted, "the fox said that we should find one another in a very ancient way."

For a moment April did wonder: he's not had a stroke has he? There would have been incoherence, said her Manager later.

"Tell stories," he said.

"What?"

"In the time of plague," continued Wilf.

"So start now," snapped Cookie, despite herself.

Well, he suggested, suppose they'd been in the house in the summer of 1940, when Stukas attacked the radar station on top of the Downs. He made the screaming noise of the dives. Some bombs fell short and hit the town. Then a pilot baled out and landed in the rose bed. They phoned the police, took him into the kitchen and made him a cuppa. Then what?

"Grab his parachute," said April. "It'll make gorgeous knickers."

AN ORDINANCE FOR THE UTTER SUPPRESSING AND ABOLISHING OF ALL STAGE PLAYS AND INTERLUDES: FEBRUARY 11 1648

"Whereas the Acts of Stage-Plays, Interludes and Common Players, condemned by Ancient Heathens, and much less to be tolerated among Professors of the Christian Religion is the occasion of many and sundry great vices and disorders, tending to the high provocation of God's wrath and displeasure, which lies heavy upon this Kingdom, and to the peace thereof…"

Dolly stopped reading. Mr Lowin gestured. Go on.

"It says that if you're caught acting you're subject to punishment as a rogue, not—"

She stumbled over a long word.

"Notwithstanding…" supplied Mrs Lowin.

"Notwithstanding any licence from the King, or any person or persons…"

"What else is required?"

"Er … to pull down and demolish or procure to be pulled down and demolished all Stage Galleries, Seats and Boxes, erected or used, or which shall be erected and used for acting, or playing, or seeing acted or played, such Stage Plays, Interludes and Plays aforesaid, within the said City of London and Liberties thereof…"

OUT OF SHAMPOO

There were confusions. Cookie agreed to tell her parents where she was but their phones were on answer and her message not returned. "There you are," she said, "nobody cares." Wilf doubted this. Despite everything he and Cookie's father Roger had always rubbed along. He thought that Roger would be civil and reply. And what calls or texts had Cookie received but not revealed?

"Just let her feel safe," said April.

"But where's she been living? Her possessions etcetera. Where are they?"

April was irritated and Wilf said "Okay. I'll be patient. But you're not very relaxed yourself, are you? What's happened?"

Her younger son. He had sneaked her credit card and run up money to buy extras for a video game. When she found out she confiscated his control gear. There were shouting matches. April's Manager deplored video games. They should be censored. No use in that, thought Wilf, when even the censor's brain has been rotted by the education system and by Woke and Twitter and West End musicals – which explanations of a cultural situation seemed even to him to be a shorthand conflation, so that all he said was "Hmmm ..." and changed the subject. What did Cookie do all day, upstairs and on her own? Write, she always said, and Wilf nodded approval. April knew that more than once Cookie had sneaked out to find Jarvis and buy dope from him, but said nothing.

Later Wilf sat on his own, wrapped in a duvet. When you're old there is less oxygen in the body and you feel colder, they had told him. He stared at bare branches and talked to himself. The house seemed cavernous. At twilight Cookie appeared and said that she'd run out of shampoo and could she have a beer?

"That's a sure sign of military collapse," he said.

"What?"

"When the officers use champagne as shaving water ..."

Non-sequiturs, but like glow-worms, somehow. She wanted to tell her older woman would-be seducer about him.

"And it's your turn to tell a story," he said.

"I'm not ready. I need more time."

"Tomorrow?"

"Maybe."

She's about to trust me, he thought, and said "Okay. Shall we make scrambled eggs and then I'll read you my Sleep-Out idea?"

WET SPRING

Mr Lowin said "You've got to make yourself heard so we'll work on this big speech outside."

But what with rain rain rain the fields were so marshy I got stuck and he had to fetch someone to pull me out and we continued in the parlour.

"Stop sweeping! Stop sweeping Dolly Sweep! Stop waving your arms about!"

Was I? I was Cleopatra on her day bed. How could I be waving my arms?

"Wave your arms for no reason and the audience don't listen to you. Why not? Because they wonder: is waving your arms what the story's about. Is it?"

"Not yet, Mr Lowin."

"No."

"I am learning, though. You're a very good teacher, Mr Lowin."

"It's the same when you jig from foot to foot."

I couldn't help it. I came out with a rhyme.

> When you're on stage don't jiggle your wrist
> Whatever you say the audience has missed

Although I have to say, all these years later, that as Mr Burt says the characters we play do more wrist-fluttering and leaning forward to show their tits than Mr Taylor managed farts. Not that I ever heard him release many, to be honest. And on the very day I was stuck in the mud he did send a message: never mind the King and the old days, we must do something to save ourselves.

SLEEP-OUT

Wilf was at one end of the sofa, with his duvet, and Cookie at the other. "I'll read the intro first," he said, and began—

'In a silk shirt to give him the edge that in financial P.R. can make the difference, Warren summoned the confidence to make it seem that the idea came to him during the meeting itself, and was inspired by something said by the most important person on the Bank's side of the table. Since the Crash, the executives admitted, our image is in freefall. People have this idea that banks and their greed are the cause. So the question is: what can we do to make ourselves seem altruistic?

Cue Warren. He rapped his pencil end on the table to signify a brain-flash. "Why not—?" he began.

Reach out? To their customers? They already did.

"No, no," said Warren. "Not to them. To the lost and lonely."

There was a silence, in which they wondered if he'd lost his marbles.

"Don't advertise," said Warren. "Campaign."

Campaign?

"Raise money for the Homeless ..."

What?

"Sponsored Sleep-Outs," he expanded. "At every Branch the staff spends a night outside, sleeping rough. Then Head Office matches the money raised pound for pound."

Cost?

"Well. Let's face it. Less than shooting a series of commercials."

So they bought it. We'll fast-track it, they said, and did. For Warren it was the breakthrough. He became a legend, and bought a much bigger house in Weybridge. '

*

"Weybridge," nodded Cookie. "Perfect."

"You mean you don't think it's daft?"

"How did you get the idea?"

Wilf began to explain but had to interrupt himself.

"Sorry. The loo. My diuretics ..."

CLERKENWELL PUMP

Wet spring and wetter summer. Another failed harvest. Harder living and no agreement between the defeated King, the Army and the dithering Parliament. And Mr Lowin dithering, until one day he sent Dolly for me and Charlie and said "Your old acting friend Will Beeston. We reckon he's the man. I've agreed to meet him at the Devil's Tavern."

It was on Fleet Street, a warren of low ceilings, side-rooms and tobacco fug, where before the War drinkers might ask actors they recognised to recite favourite speeches, which was done for a buttered ale, or a shilling, maybe, if you gave a whole scene. And it still bustled, potboys calling, songs in one snug, dice in another, but not so much your pre-War gentry, Will Beeston informed us out of the side of his stubble, as new moneymen here and lawyers bickering there, and that man, see him, straitened times of course but hopes for better: he's a spice importer and has a talking bird from far away.

"I had a goldfinch once," said Charlie. "D'you remember?"

We were joined by Mr Wadlow the publican, low-voiced and quick-eyed, and settles had been arranged so that we could not be overheard. Mr Wadlow and Will were prompted by Mr Lowin to tell tales about their fathers.

"And Mr Jonson," he said. "He valued them both, did he not?"

Mr Jonson. According to many, the greatest man of the last

age. I saw him when I was a child actor. He was genial and lumbering, a dangerous big bear who could speak Latin.

"Well," said Mr Wadlow. "Mr Jonson got the idea that my grandmother had known your street jugglers at Clerkenwell Pump, and seen your Passion plays on Cornhill, and he wanted to hear about them."

"Her memory was that good?"

"Very bad."

Laughter, and me and Charlie had heard it all before but loved to hear it again. How the theatre had become the rage all over the country, for high born and low. How actors who were shareholders in a company could make fortunes. The time Mr Pollard fell off the stage. Rivalries. Betrayals. Drunk writers not delivering on time. Hired men in the smaller parts. Italian musicians. Fights in the audience. Rotten fruit thrown and we'd all been hit by it. Closures in plague years, and who died of it. Tos and fros with the Censor. Summer touring and women loved and left in places such as Plymouth. Carpenters who worked for the Revels office. The Queen and her ladies acting in glorifying spectacles, and was Mr Inigo Jones a Welsh idiot who thought the scenery more important than the words, or was he—

Mr Wadlow was called to attend to deliveries at the alley door.

We were silent. Then Mr Lowin sighed and said "And so for the future..?"

"The Cockpit's yours when you want it," said Will Beeston, who had inherited it from his father.

Hands were shaken, and on our way out someone who had seen Mr Lowin's original performance as Volpone stopped him to ask about Mr Jonson. As we waited Charlie said "You realise what Beeston meant earlier?"

"What?"

"When he said that there's money to be borrowed."

I did not understand.

"All the royal monopolies are abolished. So if you can manage to trade abroad it's for huge profits."

"What's that to do with Beeston?"

"He wants to borrow and buy more theatres."

More theatres, when politicians intend to abolish them? Even for cocksure Will this seemed a bit – Then it struck me. Come real peacetime, whatever happened to plays and acting, bricks and mortar would rise in value.

MELODY

"It's gone humid," said Wilf, and tried to bend his fingers. "My arthritis …." He did not add that it had stopped him buttoning his flies, which he hoped she would not notice. He grabbed the duvet and explained that a Sponsored Sleep-Out had happened, and been described to him by the Bank Manager. "So I thought bingo!" he said, and read on.

'"What about toilet breaks?" was the question asked by female members of the staff and the Branch Manager Ken Babcock resolved it by saying that they would doss down not on the Quayside (in the Middle Ages important but now a weekender's Marina) where actual rough sleepers were likely to be found, but outside the Bank itself, so that people could go in as necessary.

"That won't be the true experience, though, will it?" said Ken's deputy Dan Reynolds. He was a Labour voter, and his Auntie Velma had been a Greenham Common protester.

"I see where you're coming from," said Ken, "but it's not about us. It's about raising the money."

Sometimes he and Dan bickered about Greenham Common. "I mean," Ken would say, "Gorbachev ended the Cold War and I'm not sure that Greenham Common influenced him …"

On the Sleep-Out night it rained but they stuck it out, some like young Michael in a big cardboard box, others in sleeping bags and someone under her father's golf umbrella. Passers-by stopped to chat and several gave Ken their small change. One person thought they were real and said that they should give up drugs and find proper jobs. Actual pushers, expensively sneakered and hooded, slunk by with smirks because they recognised at least one weekend customer. Late fast-foodies offered chips. A drunk started to piss on them but was scrambled away. The police passed. "Everything in order, Mr Babcock?"

Then it was quieter, and darker as timers cut off shop lights. In the wet cold it was hard to find comfortable postures. Mutters. Giggles. Lavatory coming and goings. Ken was still addressed as Mr Babcock. A fox crossed the other side of the square.

Sometimes shouts drifted up from the actual rough sleepers on the Quay, and what they had thought were garbage bags left outside a café was actually a person, they realised. Rain re-started.

Then a voice said "Sorry. Can I be with you?"

It was a girl, aged about sixteen and shivering. She had known for a week that she was pregnant. She told her boyfriend but he said that it wasn't him. That night, interrupting their argument about money, she had told her parents. They said that she was disgusting, and had always made them look ridiculous. They threw her out, and all the Council House neighbours heard the row.

"Take this groundsheet," said Ken. "What's your name?"

"Melody," she said. '

Using the Cockpit itself might have drawn attention before we needed it, and so the other actors joined us in Covent Garden. Mr Lowin, whose legs were achy, was the first to arrive, with half a bag of coal on a handcart pushed by Dolly Sweep. We made a breakfast of heated up nettle porridge, which as everyone knows is good for the lungs.

Then Rob Shatterel appeared. He would play the Queen, for which he was too young. Next came Mr Taylor, too old now for the character he had created twenty years earlier, but who cared? His hair was white but as always he seemed taller than he was. And he still had worries.

"The street's full of soldiers," he said.

"Billeted," said Charlie.

"They recognised me."

"Never …"

"They knew who I was."

"They're cavalry from up North," said Mr Lowin. "They don't know anybody."

"Didn't they recognise you?"

"I arrived on a handcart."

"We could be arrested for just sitting here," persisted Mr Taylor.

"Pardon me," interrupted Dolly Sweep, "but what I think it is, is that they're not used to seeing very handsome well-dressed people …"

"What?"

"So they would stare at you."

"For certain," said Mr Lowin with a wink at Charlie. "That's it."

"You think so?"

"Who looks twice at me?" said Dolly.

"Well. Yes. I suppose that could be it," said Mr Taylor. "Well spotted."

"Any time, Mr Taylor," said Dolly.

Mr Taylor sat down, and said that yes, he would have a bowl of nettle porridge, and what we young men should realise was that it helps an actor's lungs. He surveyed the room, realised from its furnishings that the absent owners must be wealthy, and said "Very Italianate …"

Then he asked about Mr Lowin, and Mr Lowin asked about Mr Taylor's daughters and we all watched Mr Taylor as he breathed deeply between each mouthful of porridge. Then he said "Tom Pollard not here yet, I see. Not difficulties again, are there?"

"I was waiting for you to ask that," said Mr Lowin.

Mr Taylor's eyebrows stayed up.

"But he's not farted yet," muttered Charlie behind the back of his hand.

Mr Lowin gestured at Dolly: say what we've heard.

"Well, the word is, Mr Taylor, that Mr Pollard has a much younger new gentleman friend."

Mr Taylor shrugged. So what's the difficulty?

"He's a trooper in Cromwell's Eastern Association Cavalry."

"What?"

"He thinks the theatre's the work of the Devil," said Charlie.

"How can a religious maniac be a fat old actor's boyfriend?"

"Very easily," said Mr Lowin.

"I suppose you're going to say now," said Mr Taylor, "that in a very long lifetime you've seen it all …"

"I have."

"Such as Mr Shakespeare forget his lines in that play by Mr Jonson …"

"And Mr Jonson be bloody mad at him. Yes …"

The unspoken question was if Mr Pollard was rendered unavailable, who would play his part? But it was soon answered by a hammering at the door. Rob went to answer and in bounced Mr Pollard himself, pink and flustered, and struck a pose to deliver lines from the play.

A hot day, a hot day, vengeance hot, boys.
Give me some drink, this fires a plaguey fret

He snatched Mr Taylor's porridge bowl, scooped what remained, and continued.

Body a me, I am dry still. Give me Jack, boy.
This wooden skiff holds nothing ...

He lobbed bowl and spoon and all at Rob, and kissed the top of Mr Taylor's head.

"Joseph darling. Ha ha. He he. How are you? Uneasy as ever?"

"And you?"

"I'm in love."

"Which is not always cheerful, is it, Mr Pollard?" said Dolly.

"You're a girl, Dolly, so you understand."

"Does your new lad know that you're here?" said Mr Taylor.

"Rough soldiers, Joseph. Big boots and breastplates. D'you know what I mean?"

"Having shared Tiring Rooms with you for half a lifetime, yes, I'm afraid I do."

"What I can tell you is that it's nasty. The cavalry haven't been paid."

"We know," said Mr Lowin.

"So I took the risk. 'Sweetheart,' I said to him, 'I'll see to it.' 'How?' he said. 'Acting,' I said."

We should not have been surprised but we were. There was a silence.

"Do his officers know?" said Mr Taylor.

"Joseph, what's to know is that I can make a bit to send home to his mother. I hope. He killed three men at the Battle of Naseby. He's a very dear person ..."

He sniffed, and swallowed his emotion.

"Sorry," he said. "Ha ha. He he ..."

We heard the clatter of the soldiers in the street. Mr Lowin banged the floor with his stick and said "No more chatter. Time. Have you all got your parts?"

CARDBOARD BOXES

Wilf waited for Cookie's reaction. She began to speak, stopped, smiled to herself, and re-started.

"Didn't you say before that it was a play?" she said.

"Well. Yes. Originally that was – I mean – but ..."

He explained. It was years ago and for years before that things had been different and – Just state simple facts and think about them anew, he told himself. There was inflation world-wide. Thatcher's government did not increase artistic subsidies to match. Which is true, and the Leftie explanation, but not the whole story. Something had changed in people themselves, something indifferent and careless, and it meant that the appetite for drama was different and – For the first time, he realised, she was engaged by his puzzlement at the history.

Then she said "At the same time, I mean, I'd never have seen it as television. I'd see it on stage. Well, promenade, actually. The audience has to sit in cardboard boxes or lie on the floor and ..."

Excitement. Each one's thoughts tumbled over the other's.

Don't spoil it, thought Wilf. It's her turn next.

BABYLON ON MR LOWIN'S DOG'S ARSE

The soldiers realised that we were actors, but did they know that we were rehearsing? Some were impressed by us, and chatted. What had it been like to act before the King, and was the Queen really hump-backed, and how did we remember our lines and where could they find cheap tobacco? Some sneered and called us bum-boys, and others were earnest and said in all pity cast the blindness from your eyes. Consider your soul's eternity and God's displeasure at your trade. And some asked how come we had coal when they must smash furniture and burn it?

True, we did see in their eyes our own battlefield shame and exhaustion but more often it was their anger, the anger of the wretched that was ancient and dumb, but had begun to learn how to speak, and with a force that their generals were hard put to contain.

In the Piazza preachers said prepare, prepare, prepare yourselves for Babylon to fall and the world to turn on its axis, and never be the same again.

"What they know about Babylon," said Mr Lowin, "I could write on my dog's arse!"

"You don't have a dog, though, Mr Lowin," chimed Dolly Sweep, "not at the moment," and made one of her daft rhymes.

If I was a dog and you were a cat
And tall Mr Burt was a mouse
I'd go yap-yap and you'd scratch this and that
And we'd scamper all over the house

Which was how we frolicked, full of the energy of rehearsing, and not heeding much else.

WARREN IN LOCKDOWN

Then in mid-discussion of how could they integrate music into the sleep-out, and how should it develop, because a story could end on the word 'Melody' but the dramatic narrative could not, another thought halted Cookie.

"What?" said Wilf.

"Warren ..."

"Ah. Well. You see – What day was it? You and April were online for the supermarket delivery and I—"

He had jotted a glimpse of Warren and his family today and in lockdown. So he read it.

'"My life's ruined! My entire life!" yelled Petal, who was Warren and Samantha's eldest daughter.

"No it isn't!"

"Why can't you understand?"

Door slam.

"Stupid cow!" shouted her brother.

"Fuck you!" echoed Petal.

Warren appeared from his den and said "I'm trying to check out this place in the Louberon for us so can you all please ..."

"Just shut up and uncork this bottle," said Samantha.

"Should you be doing red in the daytime?"

"Oh, you've actually noticed, have you?"

There were three vehicles in the driveway, and the house was worth three point six million.

Try, he mouthed at his son. Women. Don't set them off. Dodge round it.

Okay. I know. I know. Okay.

On Warren's phone the alarm buzzed. Shit. Zoom meeting. Get a decent shirt on. He chose a Charvet. It had been a perk from Petal's bloody awful birthday in Paris.

*

Again Wilf waited. "Well," said Cookie, "it's a sort of top and tail."

"Impossible to sell, though," said Wilf.

"Does that matter?"

It did not, they decided.

"But isn't Warren the result of the change," said Cookie, "and isn't what you wanted to show the change in society itself: and why?"

"Yes. That's where I'm stuck," said Wilf.

"Well. I'm too young. I don't know enough about it."

"But you resent something. You feel that you were born into a poor deal."

"I suppose."

Silence. They had a nightcap, Wilf's first for three weeks. "I do try," he said. "There is less pain in my legs."

REHEARSING THE MURDER SCENES

We had last done the play during the War, at Oxford, and Mr Lowin had kept the Part Books. So we were secure in our lines but had unsafe memories of the moves, especially those in the royal murder scenes. Mr Lowin, with, I surmise, a presentiment of what might happen, decided to spend a day on them: the first murder in the morning, and in the afternoon the second.

Rollo the Duke of Normandy (Mr Taylor) kills his younger brother Otto (Charlie Hart) to gain sole power. Their mother (Rob Shatterel) attempts to shield Otto but fails. That is the first murder. The second is that of Rollo himself, who in revenge for Otto's death is killed by Hammond, the Captain of the Guard.

I played Rollo's henchman Latorch. We put down our books and used walking sticks and firewood as swords and daggers. Mr Taylor showed his worry about his own lines, or so I thought, by insisting that I showed I knew mine, so we did a muttered private run-through of the scene in which Rollo screws himself up to kill.

"Why should this trouble you?" I began.

"It does, and must do, until I find ease."

"What fool would give a storm ease to disturb his peace when he may shut the casement etcetera etcetera ..."

"Conscience, Latorch. What's that?"

"A fear they tie up fools in. Nature's coward paling the blood and chilling the full spirits with apprehension of mere dark and shadows ..."

"I fear no conscience, nor I fear no shadows ..."

But from the way he was I knew that he meant to raise his famous doubts, as Mr Lowin had suspected, and so he did.

Halfway through the actual scene he jabbed Rob with his walking stick and Rob, with Charlie clinging behind him, said "I forget how we managed this, Mr Lowin," and Mr Lowin said "You do one shuffle right and then one shuffle left" and Mr Taylor interrupted. "I'm sorry. Forgive me. But as with the second murder—"

"We're not killing you yet," snapped Mr Lowin, "we're killing Otto."

"But what happens in that scene refers to this, surely?"

"Stop."

"What?"

"Joseph," said Mr Lowin, "how many times have you played this part?"

"Over the years?"

"Yes."

"A good few."

"Was it always successful?"

"Always," conceded Mr Taylor.

"Universally popular?"

"Universally."

"People stopped you on the highway to shake hands?"

"They did."

"In the taverns they bought you sack-possets and asked you to repeat speeches?"

"They did."

"Because they loved the play ..."

"Yes."

"But you always had a niggle about it."

"Increasingly."

"Joseph," said Mr Lowin, "if we act some of your murder now will you promise never to speak about this again, as long as we all shall live?"

Mr Taylor was amused, bless him.

"Yes."

There was general relief.

"With the proviso that in an extremity ..."

Laughs and comic groans...

"Agreed," said Mr Lowin.

"My arse," muttered Dolly Sweep, "but I'm learning a lot from this."

"Where d'you want to go from?" said Mr Lowin, and since the actors in the second scene had not been called until afternoon waved at Rob and me "You be Edith and you be Hammond ..."

When we had scrambled for Parts and found our places Mr Taylor said "Well. The situation replicates the murder of Otto, doesn't it? I'm lured into a room by Edith, the woman I want to marry. But she's in league with Hammond who comes in to kill me. And as Otto used our mother as a shield, I use Edith."

"Yes," said Mr Lowin.

"I have a sword. He has a knife."

"Yes."

We assumed our positions. Mr Taylor grabbed Rob around the midriff and nodded to cue me.

"Put her away," I read.

"I will not. I will not die so tamely."

"Murderous villain, wilt thou draw seas of blood upon thee?"

"Fear not," read Rob. "Kill him, good Captain, any way

dispatch him. My body's honoured with the blood that through one sends his black soul to hell."

"Shake him off bravely."

"He's too strong. Strike him."

"This is what I mean, you see," said Mr Taylor, stepping out of character. "In the first murder I tell Latorch to walk behind our mother and kill Otto."

Mr Lowin waited.

"If he did walk behind them," continued Mr Taylor, "and if they turned to face him, I could stab Otto in the back myself."

Mr Lowin tried to speak, but –

"And in the second murder, being ruthless, wouldn't I—"

Mr Taylor shoved Rob into me and as I tried to recover my balance stabbed me with his stick of firewood.

"That's not what's written," said Mr Lowin.

"But isn't it what would happen?" said Mr Taylor. "Isn't the writing stupid and false?"

Rob and Charlie and me did not know what to say, but Mr Lowin did.

"I know, Joseph. Hamlet. The death of Mercutio. Mr Webster's very truthful Italian daggers. A long time ago. Different plays in a different theatre."

"Carelessness," said Mr Taylor, "and we were very happy to ignore it and have the work."

"The audience, old friend. Changing times."

They smiled at each other, old men who knew what was beyond them. Then Mr Taylor gave a very deliberate fart and said "So rehearse us, and pray extremity never comes."

We put down one set of Part Books and picked up another, and Dolly Sweep muttered. She wasn't sure what it was about but knew it was something.

189

LOCKDOWN SUMMER

From the edge of the garden the town tumbled. Victorian villas. Balconies facing the sea. Holiday lets empty. No traffic noise. Cramped little ordinary streets out of sight. The water shimmered. Gulls clamoured over shoals. On some days there were dolphins.

MR MILTON AT WHITEHALL PALACE

Oh, to relive time and absorb it more profoundly! But we cannot, of course. The day was icy and I cold within my cloak and the Palace as blank as a ruin, untidy, plaster soggy with damp, hangings ripped down, dirty, smelling not of sweet oils and candles but of urine and stale bread and I remembered my travels and that Palace of the Barberini in Rome, where I heard the opera that was sung before scenic panels by Bernini himself, and afterwards I had talked in Latin with men whose theology I deplored, sure that it obscured God, but whose seriousness and urbanity were inspirations.

"Wait here," said the officer, and as I did I compared those men in Rome and their renewal of ancient forms and wisdoms with England's rustic barbarity, the struggle of our poesy to be itself, because I knew why I had been sent for and—

"Please," said the officer, and beckoned me into the chamber.

There was a wood fire and afternoon lanterns and in their glow upon the paintings stacked without thought, some frames chipped, some canvas rent, all dusty, I thought I saw a Tiziano. Beyond it, at a table littered with what must have been books from the King's Library, General Cromwell sat with a paper in his hand, and listened to a clerk's explanation, so that for an instant I saw him not politically composed for our meeting, but a-wrestle with his ignorance of all this art, that must be sold to pay for the army, and with his doubts and wondering what God wanted.

Can the anomalies we feel and all the nuances we see ever be recalled and re-ordered in one poem, I wondered, and then he saw me and friendship flickered across his ugly face as he re-took command and said "Mr Milton, God's grace upon you, sir," and I said "And upon you, General," and he motioned me to sit by him.

Did we make small talk about my wife, and about some excellent mincemeat that Mrs Cromwell had sent up from Ely? I think we did, and that a mouse scuttled, at which the officers at the other end of the table smiled, and men came in with more firewood and in that pause the General said "I need your knowledge as a writer, Mr Milton, to make me secure in my own mind. This excitement over the actors …"

"They're old men," I said. "Their times are hard. They need money."

"They were the King's Company. His servants."

"They were."

"They went with him to Oxford. The young ones were in his Army."

"I'm sure that all it means now," I said, "is that they were very good actors. His Majesty could, after all, buy the best."

We were aware of the stacked paintings.

"The play," said Cromwell. "It's called what?"

I waited.

"The Bloody Brother," said one of the officers.

I had heard as much myself. It was a popular melodrama, I remembered and explained, based on the murder of his younger brother, and in front of their mother, by the Roman Emperor Caracalla. For some reason John Fletcher had changed the names and set the story in the Dukedom of Normandy. There were comic scenes and a sub-plot written by Phillip Massinger.

"Both writers are dead now?"

"Yes."

"Why did the actors choose this play?"

"It's always made money."

He studied me.

"And the parts. They're supposed to show the actors to advantage."

"You mean: there's no political equivalence: no implication: no other motive?"

"I'm sure not," I said.

Cromwell pondered. He breathed in and out and said "We are under God's guidance about to put the King on trial for High Treason ..." and like a sword-thrust: "What about the audience?"

"The Cockpit's an indoor theatre. It's twice as expensive to get in. There may be some things to regret about the audience but ..."

I gestured. He waited.

"There won't be many apprentices or watermen on the one hand or country gentry on the other. There'll just be your middling city sorts who think that it's an opportunity to see old favourites ..."

Pollard would play the cook again, I had heard. I remembered the pathos beneath his obviousness.

"And the things to regret?" asked the General.

"There is an old improper jest, sir," I said, "that prostitutes were so often in the theatre that they knew the words better than some of the actors."

The officers managed not to laugh, and "Mr Milton," smiled the General, "I'm most obliged. What happens will happen. I'll not worry myself over the actors. May I walk you to the yard?"

On our way he amused me by recalling that he had acted in a play himself once, but not enjoyed it, when he was a boy at Huntingdon Grammar School.

"Doctor Beard?" I asked. The irascible Headmaster, who wrote polemical plays in his day.

"How like you to know ..." said the General.

The hackney they had sent for me now took me home, where my wife embraced me tightly, as though I had been in danger.

THE BINGO CALLER

One evening April surprised them by knocking on the conservatory glass and saying could she come in and tell a story? Yes, they said. What is it? It was about teenage lovers who went night fishing off the Island but were pulled into the sea by a mermaid, who took them to an underwater holiday camp. She'd made it up a long time ago, she said, when her elder son was a toddler with chickenpox, and originally it wasn't teenage lovers but her son's teddy bear and his friend who was a stuffed zebra. The zebra had food fads, to which Wilf said "Crikey, that fat girl I knew was like that. Runny nose. Always."

The holiday camp bingo caller was a walrus, said April.

COCKPIT

Why cry? People said. You'll forget it. Why cry, and if you do don't wipe your nose on your sleeve, a very bad habit that skivvies can get into. And if you don't forget it, well, one day you'll laugh and get over it but I never did, I never have and I never will because it was the worst, it was like having your head shoved down a privy, it was – and what was the sickest was that it made you realise about yourself and about other people. And it wasn't the blank in the eyes of a wicked person. I've seen that, men and some women as well, to spite you, but it wasn't that because it was deliberate. It was smiling, even, and as sure as sure as sure that they were right and everybody else was wrong.

I mean, it wasn't even like what Mr Burt and Charlie say the War was like, a sort of honest anger and everybody frightened underneath. It wasn't that. It was the way they looked at you. You were of no meaning. You weren't even piss, you weren't even—

Which is why "Dolly," said Mrs Lowin, "has taken it as bad as anyone," which is to say I'd been a stupid girl and thought I could whizz and dance and cheek my way out of anything and—

And what? What am I talking about? I'm talking about the fourth day at the Cockpit Theatre when soldiers stopped the performance, slapped and shoved the audience, smashed the seating, pissed and shat on the Tiring-Room floor, ripped the baize and arrested the actors. I kicked at one's shin, slipped, fell down and got up again and tried to scratch him but he punched me in the mouth and cried "Blasphemer! Witch! Blasphemer! No plays! No Babylon! God's will be done!"

QUESTIONS AND ANSWER

In pain, unable to sleep and up early, Wilf sat in the conservatory with a fruit juice and heard birdsong. He closed his eyes and saw a walrus boom bingo numbers. Harpooner's Line. Ninety and Nine. Then he heard footsteps and a chair plonked and Cookie said "Sorry. Can't wait until tonight and don't need a story. Are you my grandfather?"

"No," he said. "I'm afraid I'm not."

"Oh."

He waited.

"But the day I arrived," she said. "You did think I was someone else."

"Yes."

"My grandma Janet?"

"Yes."

"Were you in love with her?"

"Who said that I was?"

"Rumours. Cousins. Overheard their mother."

"Not the rest?"

"Oh, the rest just mutter that you betrayed the entire family."

"I did."

She hesitated. The New Model Army, he thought. Was God present at the campfires? Can this girl give me absolution?

"They began on the moors," he said. "Handloom weavers. Then no work and down to the valley and the mills. My grandfather was eight years old and crawled under machines, and all the sacrifices to make money and be respectable. Can you imagine how proud they were to be able to send me to boarding school, and then I made it to Cambridge and …"

Waving his arm. And all the rest, and everything we've sniped about.

"But they didn't like what you'd become," she said.

"I did behave badly."

"So have I."

"Although I never wrote about them."

"I did."

"I loved them. It would have been wrong to hurt them."

But would it, he thought. And, oh God, but she's like her.

She is her. She's refused to die.

"What?" said Cookie. "Why are you staring?"

"I loved her but failed her," he said, "in the most cowardly and insulting and unforgiveable way, and the longer I live the more it sickens me."

Cookie wanted to speak but did not.

"It's the woman who has everything to protect, isn't it," he said, "and if the man lacks the courage to respond and …"

His shoulders rocked and he thought: my selfish fear again, even in this conversation. But she realised.

"You mean you were afraid she'd reject you?"

"Yes."

"So you did nothing."

"No."

"OmyGod …"

He could not look at her. Then he did.

"There are croissants," she said. "I'll make breakfast."

She moved and he followed, wanting to touch her but not doing.

She filled the kettle but left it in the sink, and opened a drawer and banged it shut, then spun, wet-eyed, her head at Janet's angle of defiance.

"But she still got pregnant, didn't she?"

"Yes."

"Which was why she and old Jeremy split?"

"Yes."

"So in her hurt she'd gone with someone else?"

The sunlight, he remembered. The very sunlight of the day he found out.

"Who?"

"I don't know."

He prayed that the lie was convincing. He looks ridiculous, she thought. He hasn't even brushed his hair. She giggled.

"What?" he said, his arms shrugged open with the question.

"Can't we pretend?" she said, and walked into the embrace, still holding knives and a spoon for the jam, and wanted nothing else. "Grand-daughter," he said. "Actual or not. Grand-daughter."

He did not tell her that he had already altered his will in her favour.

GEWGAWS OF PRETENCE

What was it some soldier shouted at me? "Your feathers and gewgaws of pretence!" as we were dragged, still in whatever stage costumes we had managed to improvise, no chance to grab our own clothes and cloaks, through the Tiring House and into the fog and frozen mud. We did glimpse Dolly Sweep with a bloody face and Charlie yelled "Mr Taylor's daughter!" at her. But where was Beeston? Safely away with the gate-money we discovered later, but at the time it was stumbling down Drury Lane and up Fleet Street, a drummer beating, people staring, some jeering, none daring to shout support, most sullen, and I realised that I was speaking my lines to myself as though I was in the next scene and still have in my memory a final picture of Mr Taylor acting, his extraordinary truthfulness, and beyond him the commotion of the audience trying to get out and soldiers holding pikes crossways to push and disrupt. Then we were hustled past Pilgrim Lane and did the feather merchants still work there and – And we must have passed the Devil Tavern without me noticing and had Mr – and I felt humiliated as I suppose was the intention.

THE WONDER BOOK OF SOLDIERS

Then Wilf and Cookie talked about themselves. If Cookie had been born at the same time as Wilf, would she think as he did about things? And if he was her age would he, if he was a girl, text twenty-five times a day as every feeling changed, or if he was a boy send unasked-for pictures of his penis? She still received such, admitted Cookie, and with added insults because they had realised she was gay. Who were 'they' Wilf wanted to know, but she was vague; and having found Wilf's miles of bookshelves, and going through them daily like Customs men doing a rummage, she read and read and paid less attention to the little screen.

Which suited Wilf. It was often easier to sit with his eyes closed, because his legs hurt, cramp-like spasms when he tried to walk, and sometimes he felt his heart's weakness. This was not so much a pain as a presence, like a sponge inside him that tried to squeeze itself. Many heart attacks occur at night, the doctor had said, and Wilf thought: I could die at any time and I don't care and I realise that the panic that impelled me to foolish acts and utterings was about obliteration. Things that when I'm dead no-one else will ever know. Not things about me, so much, but things that should be passed on, things that might remind and illuminate. Things that were just there, as moments in life. Things about Frances. About the way it was in the studio when TV plays were live. What everyone knew and how they felt. I mean, what had it been like at the Globe Theatre when they played 'Hamlet' on a late Spring afternoon? How much of the stage could Burbage see as he waited to come on? Or did he have to hear the cue?

He did say some of this to Cookie and she was interested and said "Women's lives are like that all the time," and he said "What?" and she said "Like you now. Anticipating."

Which he knew now he had failed to understand for most of his life. And she fetched one of his books and laid it in front of him. It was old and broken-backed. THE WONDER BOOK OF SOLDIERS. The cover picture was of a British officer in gaiters and puttees, a Smith and Wesson revolver in his hand and a Union Jack behind him.

"Did you really believe," she said, "all this patriotic rubbish?"

"Half of it was true," he said. "Wasn't it?"

She showed him the fly leaf. The first owner's name was written in a child's hand. KATHLEEN SCHOFIELD FEB 27 1926.

"Before I was born," he said. But he remembered her.

"They gave books like this to girls?"

"Certainly," he said. "How many noble ideals do people you know have? If any?"

It was a stone holding-cell with a pail to shit in and nowhere to sit except the floor. There were two cutpurses there, and a drunk who lay on his back and moaned. Mr Taylor had lost a shoe and his foot bled, but he sat upright against the wall, aloof and somehow vindicated. One of our hired actors spat abuse at the soldiers about Cromwell, but they jeered back that they did not need officers to tell them what to do, nor how at the coming end of the world God would decide. Mr Lowin seemed shattered, no longer a bulky force, but shapeless and crumpled, all belly-flop and wheeze. He muttered to himself as Rob Shatterel cried "Good heart, lads! Good heart!" and made an attempt to sing. Mr Taylor said "Memories ..." and I said "I wish I was married," for no reason at all, and every reason in the world, and what a mockery of a memory it was, to be within a carter's spit of our Blackfriars Theatre and van Dyke's lodgings and in Hatton House itself, at whose jetty the Revels Office had loaded scenery to float upriver to Whitehall, which was to be burned in the Great Fire, the smell of piss on our prison day and of ashes later.

Did Mr Taylor read my jumble of a lost world or did I utter it? I don't remember. I never could. But what he said echoes.

"We're to blame," he said. "Ourselves. Us and all like us. How carelessly we lived, when there was shipwreck everywhere. How little we cared ..."

Which spurred some life in Mr Lowin, who after all did live the longer of the two. "Same old Joseph," he managed to grin. "Give us a pause and a what-not ..." and then there was a commotion because Dolly Sweep and Mr Taylor's eldest Hester had come with clothes and shoes for us.

The soldiers argued against admitting them but Hester was tall, and like her father seemed to have space around her. She drew respect and no-one shoved her. A bossy little civilian in black they did jostle, but he had his way and Dolly and Hester were let in and Charlie said "What happened?"

"No warrant."

"Warrant."

"They never got a warrant from a magistrate."

So we were released, although they abused us as we struggled into clothes, and Mr Pollard was weepy.

"But there are some rose petals, as you might say, Mr Pollard," said Dolly. "You'll get your money."

"Thank you," he said, and managed a "Ha ha. He he," before sniffling again.

But where next I wondered. It's ended. Where next?

"We wasted time," said Mr Taylor, "so now doth time waste us …"

A BEE BUZZED

A bee buzzed. Cookie read. Wilf lay back. His eyes were closed. He talked to himself. Cookie looked and said "What?"

I'm William Wycherley and I'm standing at the back of the pit to watch a play I've written and when the people crammed round me burst into laughter I feel this great surge of power and of being spot-on right again and if I turn my head I can see this fantastic woman in the front row of a box and she used to be the King's mistress and now I'm fucking her and it's rumpety-bump and the belly-roar of their applause and I'm the most important person there and they let me through into Charlie Hart's room backstage, where he's flushed and laughs, and drinks are poured, voices and whoops but Charlie's sad as well and I say 'Good friend what ails you?' and he says 'I am Duchess of Malfi still …'

Wilf stopped. Eyes wide. Mouth open. Cookie waited. Duchess of Malfi. A friend wanted to improvise on it. Make it properly feminist.

At which Wycherley said "What?" and Charlie said we played

to rich and poor, didn't we, all the world in the same building and on stage, and now we don't and will we ever again? I can't explain anything, really. Neither can I, said Wilf. I thought I could but I can't. I just know I lived through it and that I want you to care.

WHAT ELSE?

What else? Oh, yes. Lockdown ended and the town was swamped by people. They had a sullen, determined insistence and left their rubbish behind them on the beach. Plastic. Paper. Pizza cartons. Soiled nappies. Still hot tin foil barbecues. Tampax wrapped in wet wipes. Towels, sometimes, and dropped toys. In London a play by Wilf Maguire was cancelled because of something he'd said on television ten years earlier. Wilf and Cookie had more than one earnest discussion about someone called Melody.

"Local?" said April.

A character in a story, they said.

"Right," said April. "Aren't your prescriptions up for renewal?"

Then after intense phone-calls when she rushed into the garden so that no-one could hear (although she did once ask Wilf "What would you do?") Cookie went to meet her older woman admirer. In Winchester. Separate rooms in a B and B. Negotiating love, smiled Wilf. Wycherley and Congreve. Etcetera. Can't wait to know. But next day he wasn't up when April arrived late and there was silence and she went to where he slept and although his eyes and mouth were open he was dead.

When Frank Maguire heard he tried to write an obituary but one paper refused and another said "Thanks but we've got one on file." It was short and grudging. Disjointed facts, opined Cookie, that gave no idea of what he was like.

THE END

Lightning Source UK Ltd.
Milton Keynes UK
UKHW011130060323
418105UK00006B/958